FROM THE
NANCY DREW FILES

THE CASE: *Nancy tries to track down the thief who stole priceless jewelry from the campus museum—and clear the name of an Emerson College undergrad.*

CONTACT: *Ned's friend Rob Harper is feeling the heat, and he may end up cooling his heels in jail.*

SUSPECTS: *William Whorf—the avid jewel collector has demonstrated a deep interest in the campus museum exhibit.*

Rob Harper—he boasted of his ability to circumvent the museum's security system.

Greg Forsyte—the Emerson student has a grudge against Rob and has made no secret of his desire for revenge.

COMPLICATIONS: *Rob swears he is innocent, but every new piece of evidence seems to tighten the case against him.*

D1042881

Books in The Nancy Drew Files™ Series

Available from ARCHWAY Paperbacks

THE NANCY DREW FILES™

Case 54

COLD AS ICE

CAROLYN KEENE

AN ARCHWAY PAPERBACK
Published by POCKET BOOKS
New York   London   Toronto   Sydney   Tokyo   Singapore

AN ARCHWAY PAPERBACK *ORIGINAL*

An Archway Paperback published by
POCKET BOOKS, a division of Simon & Schuster

1230 Avenue of the Americas, New York, NY 10020

Copyright © 1990 by Simon & Schuster Inc.
Produced by Mega-Books of New York, Inc.

ISBN: 0-671-70031-6

First Archway Paperback printing December 1990

10 9 8 7 6 5 4 3 2 1

NANCY DREW, AN ARCHWAY PAPERBACK and
colophon
are registered trademarks of Simon Schuster Inc.

THE NANCY DREW FILES is a trademark
of Simon & Schuster Inc.

Cover art by Penalva

Printed in the U.S.A.

IL 7+

COLD AS ICE

Chapter

One

"WE'RE ALMOST THERE," Nancy Drew announced. Her blue eyes sparkled with anticipation as she turned her Mustang onto the tree-lined street that led up to the Emerson College campus.

Her friend George Fayne, in the front passenger seat, said, "It was great of Ned to invite us to Winter Carnival. I love winter sports." As if to emphasize her words, George tugged on her navy ski hat, beneath which the curly ends of her dark brown hair peeked out.

From the back seat, George's cousin Bess Marvin gave a little laugh. "You like any sport, George," she said. "The thing that I'm looking forward to this weekend is the dance Saturday night. It's probably the only time all weekend that I'll be able to take off my down jacket and mittens."

"Today's only Thursday," Nancy reminded her. "That means three days of outdoor torture until the dance."

Bess groaned. She wasn't athletic at all. Boys, not sports, would always be her priority.

Nancy glanced at Bess in the rearview mirror. She admired her friend's bright blue jacket, which complemented her long blond hair and bright blue eyes. Emerson boys, look out!

Nancy wheeled the Mustang through the elaborate wrought-iron gates and on to the campus. "Ned should be waiting for us at the student center," she announced. "His friends Rob and Jerry are supposed to be there, too."

"Rob and Jerry?" George questioned. "We haven't met them on any of our other visits here, have we?"

"Who cares?" Bess said, grinning. "As long as they're cute."

Nancy laughed. "Ned says they're great. And even if they're not, you're only dating them for the dance."

After parking the car, Nancy and her friends walked across the snow-covered campus to the student center, a large, old-fashioned stone building that had once been the university president's mansion. They pushed through the carved oak doors and paused inside to look around. The entrance hall was two stories high, with wood-paneled walls and a ribbed ceiling. Through an arched doorway, Nancy could see a fire crackling in the main room's stone fireplace. The delicious aroma of french fries and hamburgers drifted out from a small grill at the far end. A few tables were clustered in that area.

"Nancy!"

Nancy felt a warm tingle at the sound of the familiar voice. She turned, already smiling, to see Ned Nickerson, her longtime boyfriend, striding toward her, a huge grin lighting up his handsome face and dark eyes. An instant later he was giving Nancy a hug that lifted her off the floor.

"It's *great* to see you," he exclaimed into her reddish blond hair. "I've missed you."

Nancy smiled mischievously. "I suppose I've missed you, too," she teased. "Hey, Nickerson, do you think you could put me down?"

Ned gently lowered her to the floor, then greeted Bess and George. "I'm glad you could come. Winter Carnival is the number-one event of the year at Emerson."

"You mean it's the only thing that makes this time of the year bearable," Nancy said.

Ned ran a hand through his dark wavy hair. "Well—let's say it helps. Come on. I want you to meet Rob and Jerry. Um, I figured that since Jerry is an enthusiastic skier, he and George would get along well. As for Rob—" He paused for a moment, and Nancy saw a troubled look pass over his face. But all he said was, "He's a great guy, too, Bess."

Nancy was curious about the look that had passed over Ned's face. She wondered if there was something he wasn't telling them about Rob. Bess hadn't seemed to notice, so Nancy decided not to make a big deal of it.

"All right!" Bess said. "Let the festivities begin!"

The three girls followed Ned into the main room, toward the couches and chairs near the fireplace. Two guys got up from a window seat and came toward them.

"Wow," Bess whispered. "Not bad, Nan."

"Shh!" Nancy cautioned. "They'll hear you." She had to admit that Bess was right, though. One of the guys had big brown eyes, dark hair combed straight back, broad shoulders, and a muscular physique. The other was taller and slimmer, with green eyes and light brown hair that fell over his forehead. Nancy didn't think either guy was as handsome as Ned—but almost.

Ned made the introductions. Jerry McEntee, the one with light brown hair, gave the girls a big smile that became warmer when he said hello to George. Rob Harper, the dark-haired guy, nodded and said hello, before looking away.

"How was your drive down?" Jerry asked George.

Bess jumped in. "It was great," she said enthusiastically. "I mean, the fresh snow made everything look soft and pretty. No sharp edges anywhere."

Turning to George, Jerry said, "Ned tells me you like to ski. Did you bring your gear?"

"Only downhill," George said. "Is that all right?"

"Sure," Ned said. "There's a place in town that rents cross-country skis, if we decide to give that a try. Listen, we ought to get you guys settled in your dorm. Then we can head down to the lake while we still have lots of light."

"Are we taking a swim?" Nancy teased. "Don't tell me Emerson is starting a polar bear club!"

Ned answered, saying, "Remember I told you about the snow sculpture contest my fraternity is sponsoring? Well, it's taking place down by the lake. We have only three days to work on our sculpture. That's not a lot of time, since we plan on coming in first place."

"Don't tell me this is one of your frat's hallowed traditions," Bess groaned. "Forcing everyone to suffer in the bitter cold."

"Not everyone's as much of a wimp about the cold as you are," George said. "Some of us actually enjoy being outside."

"Well, maybe the sculpting part will be fun," Bess conceded. Turning to Ned, she said, "The judges won't make fun of the sculptures if they're not great, will they?"

Ned straightened up indignantly. "I beg your pardon—this is serious business. We would never 'make fun' of any of it."

"We?" George repeated. "Are you a judge, Ned?"

"Not *a* judge. I'm the head judge," Ned told her.

A few minutes later, as they were carrying the bags to the dorm, Ned said, "It's pretty crowded on campus this weekend, but I managed to find a place for you to stay, with a girl whose roommate is away. There's only one free bed, though, so I guess two of you will have to make do with sleeping bags on the floor," he added apologetically.

"That's okay," George said. "Bess and I don't mind."

Bess looked at her cousin skeptically. "Hey,

speak for yourself! Well, I guess I really don't mind," she said to Ned. "It's a good thing we brought our sleeping bags."

Nancy, Bess, and George found the room where they'd be staying and knocked on the door. It was opened by a girl with dark eyes and black hair cut straight just below her ears. She was wearing a bright orange oversize sweater and jeans. "Hi. You must be Ned's friends. I'm Susan Samuels. Come on in and park your things."

"Thanks," Nancy said. "I'm Nancy Drew. And this is Bess Marvin and George Fayne." She dropped her bag and skates on the bed Susan indicated and propped her skis up in the corner next to a pair of shiny slalom skis with high-tech bindings. "We really appreciate your putting us up," she told Susan.

"Yeah, I hope we won't be keeping you from studying or anything," added George as she and Bess put their stuff down next to Nancy's.

"Studying?" Susan said, arching one eyebrow. "It's practically a crime to mention that word during Winter Carnival. At Emerson, when carnival comes, everything else stops."

Crossing to the window, Nancy stared outside. The walks had been cleared, but the lawns and the roofs were deep in snow, and icicles hung from all the eaves. Snow glistened on the branches of the trees dotting the campus lawns.

At the foot of the hill, on the other side of a small wood of evergreens, was a white expanse that glinted in the sunlight. Nancy could see the colorful parkas of people who were already working on their snow sculptures. "You have a great view," she said. "Is that the lake?"

"That's right," Susan replied.

"Which reminds me," Nancy said. "We'd better get moving. We're supposed to be down there working right now."

As the girls turned to leave, Nancy and George paused to glance at a framed photo on Susan's dresser. It was of two men in business suits cutting a ribbon in front of a store whose sign read Samuels for Sports. Susan was next to them, a big smile on her face.

"Hey, I know that place," George commented. "It's the best sporting goods store in this area."

"My father owns it," Susan said proudly. "Built it up from nothing—all on his own. In fact, it's now the largest independent sports store in the state." She turned and rummaged around on her dresser. "Let me give you a room key," she said. "I'll be in and out a lot."

"Thanks," Nancy said, zipping the key into the pocket of her parka. "I guess we'll see you later?"

"You bet," Susan replied. "I'll be down at the lake. You don't think I'm going to let you guys win the sculpture contest, do you?"

The girls said goodbye and went downstairs to meet Ned, Jerry, and Rob. They found the boys in the middle of a snowball fight, their clothes covered with the white powder.

"Ready?" Ned asked as Jerry threw a snowball that grazed his shoulder and sprayed snow over his face. "Hey!" he exclaimed. Bending over, he picked up a handful of snow and tossed it—not at Jerry, but at Nancy.

"Wha—!" Nancy sputtered, brushing the soft flakes off her face.

"Welcome to Winter Carnival," Ned said with a laugh, then ducked as Nancy fired a return snowball at him. Jerry threw a snowball at George, and for the next ten minutes the air was filled with flying snowballs and excited cries.

When they were red from the cold and dusted with snow from head to foot, the group headed down the hill to the lake. Some people were working in teams, and others on their own. Nancy admired a castle, a snowman, and what looked like an Indian village. With the other projects, it was too early to tell what they would represent.

Bess was in awe of the sculptures. "I don't know what to do," she said with a sigh.

"I'm a judge," Ned reminded her, "so I'm sorry, but I can't give you any help."

"Why don't you start by piling up a mound of

snow and seeing what comes to you?" George suggested to Bess.

Nancy glanced around her. "Maybe I'll do a model of one of the campus buildings," she said, pointing at an ultramodern structure on the bluff just above them. "Like the Emerson Museum."

"Too easy," Ned scoffed. "Five or six cubes piled on top of one another. That reminds me, I have to go to the opening of an exhibit of jewelry at the museum tonight. It should just take a few minutes, but I have to show up because of my art history course. You guys can skip it if you want."

Bess's pale blue eyes lit up. "Sounds like it might be interesting. What kind of jewelry is it?"

"A collection of rare pieces that were crafted during the seventeen and eighteen hundreds for famous celebrities, royalty, and heads of state."

"Ooh!" Bess sighed dramatically. "I can't wait to see them!"

Nancy shrugged. "I guess that settles it. We'll go with you, Ned."

Pointing a mittened thumb at her cousin, George joked, "Any excuse to get out of the cold, right, Bess?" Turning to Ned, she asked, "What else is on for the weekend?"

"Tomorrow they're dedicating the new rowing tank," Ned told her.

"What's a rowing tank?" Nancy asked.

"It lets the crew practice rowing during the

winter, when the lake is frozen. That's it over there, at the back of the boat house."

Nancy glanced over her shoulder at an old-fashioned wooden building on the far side of the lake. She remembered the boat house from earlier visits to Emerson College. Its green paint really stood out now against the snowy whiteness surrounding it, and the row of big double doors across the front were striking. The cement-walled addition at the far end of the building looked dull and lifeless by comparison.

"The addition's not very attractive," Nancy remarked. "I liked the boat house better before."

"I agree," Ned said. "But I wouldn't say that around any of the guys on the rowing team if I were you. That includes Rob. He and the other guys raised the money to build it."

"Sorry. I hope he didn't hear me." She didn't see Rob nearby. She finally spotted him standing at the edge of the lake, staring moodily across the lake toward the boat house. Good, Nancy thought. He hadn't heard her.

"Hey, Nancy," Bess called. "You're falling behind on the job. Get to work!"

Bess had already scooped a big pile of snow together and was starting to mold it. A little farther along, George and Jerry were working on the walls of a fortress.

Nancy knelt down and began to pack some of

the fluffy snow. By the time the sun set, she and the others were so cold their fingers and toes were starting to get numb, but they'd all gotten a good start on their sculptures.

"Why don't we head over to the student center and warm up," Ned suggested. "They're going to have different bands playing all weekend long."

Ten minutes later they had made their way back to the stone student center.

"Pretty good crowd," Ned said, unzipping his ski jacket. He and Nancy were warming themselves in front of the fireplace. Across the room, a piano and guitar duo was getting ready to play, but Nancy doubted that anyone would be able to hear them over the buzz of conversation.

"I'll go get us some hot cocoa," Ned said.

Nancy nodded, and Ned threaded his way through the crowd.

"Hi," came a voice from behind her. "How's your snow sculpture coming along?"

"Oh, hi, Susan," Nancy replied, turning to face her roommate. "Fine, I guess. I'm doing a snowman. Pretty basic. I didn't see you down at the lake."

Susan grimaced. "Tell me about it. I work part-time at the museum, and some things came up." She brushed a hand through her black hair. "I guess I'll get up early tomorrow to work on my sculpture."

"Brrr," Nancy said with a laugh. "That's what I call dedication. Oh, there's Bess."

She waved to Bess, who came over to join them. After saying hi to Susan, Bess said, "I seem to have lost my date. Maybe I should put you on the case, Nancy." Turning to Susan, she added, "Nancy's a detective, you know."

"An efficient one, too," Nancy teased, glancing over Bess's shoulder. "I've already solved your case! Here comes Rob now, with Ned."

Susan followed Nancy's gaze, and the smile disappeared from her face. Nancy was about to ask her what was wrong when Susan muttered darkly, *"He's* your date? Rob Harper?"

She continued to glare angrily. "If I were you, Bess, I'd watch out for that guy. He's not what he seems!" With that, she turned and walked away.

Chapter

Two

NANCY WATCHED as Susan disappeared into the crowd. What had she meant by that remark?

"What was *that* all about?" Bess demanded.

"What was what all about?" Ned asked, as he and Rob joined the girls. The guys carried mugs of steaming cocoa topped with whipped cream.

Rob grimaced, then said, "Let me guess. You were talking to Susan Samuels, and when she saw me coming, she walked away. Right?"

"That's right," Bess said. "I guess you two don't get along?"

Rob nodded. "You could say that. It's a long story."

Nancy wondered what had happened but decided it was none of her business.

George and Jerry joined them a moment later. "A band's starting to play downstairs," Jerry said. "What do you say we go down and dance?"

Bess smiled. "I'm all for that. Let's go!"

The cellar was enormous, with a wooden dance floor flanked on two sides with small tables and chairs.

"This is definitely my favorite way to warm up," Nancy told Ned as they danced to a fast song.

"Not mine," he said. Just then the band launched into a slow number, and Ned reached over to pull Nancy close to him. He bent down and whispered in her ear, *"This* is my favorite way to warm up, with my favorite girl."

Nancy's heart soared, and after several more songs she and Ned finally tore themselves away from the dance floor to join the others at a table.

"Hey, Nickerson," Jerry said. "If you're dragging us to a boring museum opening, we'd better at least go on full stomachs."

"I'll second that," Rob said. Turning to Bess, he added, "They always make some dry speech at the beginning of these events. We'll definitely need some burgers and fries to make it through alive."

* * *

A half hour later, fueled with food, the gang started across campus to the museum. The sun had set, and the trees and buildings formed dark shadowy recesses between the lights. The icy wind whistled through the bare branches as they made their way down the path.

Jerry took the lead, setting off at a fast pace, with George and Bess on either side of him. Nancy and Ned were a few steps back, just behind Rob.

"Hey, what's the big rush?" Nancy heard Bess complain.

"I want to be first in line," Jerry said, flashing a wide smile. "They might decide to give away free samples."

"I could handle that," Bess said. "Nothing too flashy, just a small pin set with diamonds and pearls."

Jerry laughed and took both girls' arms in his, explaining, "The sidewalk looks icy up ahead."

"Sure, Jerry," Rob called jokingly. "You just want an excuse to hog my date, too."

Nancy had been admiring Rob's jacket, which was dark purple wool with orange leather sleeves and crossed oars embroidered in white on the back. She tugged on Ned's arm so that they could catch up to Rob. She decided to talk with him.

"This campus is beautiful, even at night," Nancy commented, sandwiched between the two boys. "I feel as if I've walked into a photo on a greeting card."

Rob laughed. "I hardly notice anymore. I guess when you're in a place all the time, you stop really seeing it. It takes a visitor to make you appreciate it."

"That's quite a jacket you've got on," Nancy said. "Those oars on the back—they mean that you're a rower, right?"

Rob shoved his gloved hands in his jacket pockets. "Sort of," he said gruffly. He hesitated, then added, "I got the jacket after the regional regatta last year. That's the biggest crew race of the year. I pulled third oar in the boat that won the finals."

"Really? That's terrific," Nancy said. "You must have been proud."

"Yeah," he mumbled. It was clear that something was upsetting him and that he didn't want to continue their conversation. Nancy remembered how Susan had warned them about Rob. Could it have something to do with his rowing? She decided to ask Ned about it when they were alone.

When they reached the modern, cubelike museum building, they pushed through the huge metal doors.

"Not too shabby," Ned commented, studying a poster of an emerald bracelet by the entrance.

17

"Oh, it's gorgeous! Wouldn't it look great on me?" Bess said, holding out her wrist.

George gave her cousin a gentle push. "Come on, we're here to look and admire, not to take."

"The speeches are beginning," Ned said, pointing to a microphone set up at the far end of the entrance hall. A tall, thin man wearing a green turtleneck under a heavy tweed jacket was tapping on the mike.

"That's Mr. Fantella, the director of the museum," Ned whispered to Nancy.

"I'd like to welcome everyone to this marvelous exhibition," the museum director began. "I know you are eager to see this astonishing collection of historic jewels, but first I would like to introduce and thank the man who made this exhibition possible. Mr. William Whorf is a noted collector and expert on historic jewelry. He is also a trustee and generous friend of Emerson College. Mr. Whorf?"

As Nancy and the other spectators applauded, a heavyset man with a round face and wavy gray hair stepped forward. Light sparkled from a diamond ring on his little finger and a diamond stickpin in his necktie. The museum director wasn't kidding when he said Whorf likes to collect jewelry, Nancy thought.

"Thank you," Mr. Whorf said. "And don't

worry, I'm not going to make a speech. I just want to ask you to remember, as you look at this exhibition, that each and every item is unique, either because one of the world's most talented and renowned jewelers designed and made it, or because great figures in history, such as Queen Victoria of England, Catherine the Great of Russia, and Otto von Bismarck of the German Empire, owned and wore them. They are not just beautiful works of art, but a testament to some of the great figures in European history."

After another polite round of applause, the doors to the exhibit were opened. There were too many people crowded around the first few showcases for Nancy or her friends to see anything.

"Follow me," Rob said. "I know a shortcut to the other end of the exhibit. We can work our way backward."

"Ohhh," Bess said, leaning over one of the last glass display cases. "I've never seen anything so beautiful!"

Resting on a cushion of black velvet were a matched necklace, bracelets, and earrings of deep, red rubies and glittering diamonds. The rubies were larger than any Bess had seen before. They were set in gold filigree with dozens of diamonds around them.

Glancing at the typed card next to the jewelry,

Nancy said, "They used to belong to the Empress of Austria. Now they're in the collection of a museum in Vienna."

"What a shame," Bess said. "They were meant to be worn, not to sit in some cold, dusty museum. I wish I could take them home."

"Be sensible," George said. "Where would you wear something like that if you had it?"

Bess tossed her head. "I'd put them on at home and look in the mirror." She laughed. "Then I guess I'd give them back to the museum. I couldn't begin to afford the insurance premiums on them!"

As Bess leaned over for a closer look at the jewels, Nancy noticed the guard straightening up and moving slowly in their direction.

"I'd be glad to get them for you," Jerry joked, "but I'd never get away with it. The museum just put in a super new electronic alarm system."

"That shouldn't stop us," Rob said, bending over for a closer look at the case. "Anyone who knows about electronics could get past the system. I bet if you gave me ten minutes I could walk out of here with that stuff. Maybe less— maybe only five minutes."

Nancy glanced up to see the guard only a few feet away. He was listening hard and studying Rob's face as if he were trying to memorize it.

"Better watch what you say," Nancy cautioned

Rob in an undertone. "I think that guard is taking you seriously."

"Oh, look," George said, pointing to a case on the far wall. "Jeweled armor! I wonder who it belonged to."

"Some guy who cared more about his looks than about winning fights," Rob quipped.

After a half hour the six friends found themselves back in the entrance hall. "It's a great show," Bess said, "but I don't think I can look at another brooch or goblet."

"Me, too," George agreed. "Can you imagine the fortunes people spent on all that jewelry? It's amazing."

"I guess we'd better head back to our dorm. Even though it's still early, I'm tired from the long drive and the cold," Nancy said.

The walkway from the museum to the dorms was flanked by evergreens. Nancy and Ned followed the others, their feet crunching on the hard, packed snow. She made sure she and Ned were out of the others' hearing range. "Rob seemed down when I asked him about rowing earlier. Is something wrong?"

"Rob's always been a gung-ho oarsman. He probably did more than anyone else to raise money for the new rowing tank. Tomorrow's dedication ceremony is a big deal for him."

"Then why isn't he excited?" Nancy asked.

"He got a letter from the dean last week. Because of his grades, he's been put on academic probation and suspended from crew."

"Oh, the poor guy!" Nancy exclaimed.

"He's pretty bitter, too," Ned said. "He got letters from his professors this term saying his work had improved, but the dean wouldn't budge. Rob's going to miss the spring season and the big regatta in May. It's a raw deal, if you ask me."

"No wonder he didn't want to talk when I asked about his jacket," Nancy said. "I must have made him think about everything he's going to miss."

Ned shook his head. "Don't blame yourself, Nan. He thinks about it all the time anyway."

After saying good night to the guys, Nancy, Bess, and George went upstairs to Susan's room.

"I guess Susan's still out," Bess said, seeing that the room was empty.

"It was really nice of her to let us stay here," George commented as she and Bess rolled out their sleeping bags on the floor.

Nancy draped her parka over the back of the desk chair, then began to go through her bag for her nightgown. "I hope she doesn't feel uncomfortable having us here now that she knows we're friends with Rob."

"It's not like we're on anyone's side or anything," Bess added.

"Mmmm." As they drifted off to sleep, Nancy thought ahead to the next couple of days. She was thrilled to have a few days of fun with no case to worry about.

"Dedication is one thing," Bess said, shivering as she added a handful of snow to her snow castle. "But nobody said anything about getting up at seven in the morning!"

"Oh, come on. It wasn't that bad," George said. Her cheeks were bright red and her breath made a cloud in the early morning air. She was concentrating on keeping a thick, snowy wall of her fort from falling down.

"Ned said there's a lot going on today. This might be the only chance we have to work on these." She glanced at her watch. "He and Rob and Jerry ought to be here any minute."

A snowball hit Nancy in the back, and she whirled around to see Ned and the others coming toward them.

"Okay, Nickerson, you asked for it," Nancy threatened, bending to grab some snow.

He put up his hands and made a face of mock horror. "No, don't! I give up."

"Cut it out, you guys," Rob said in a serious

voice. "We have to get going if we don't want to be late for the boat house dedication."

The girls brushed the snow from their gloves, and they all set off on the snow-covered path that curved around the lake to the boat house.

It was warm inside the new cement addition, so they took off their jackets, piling them up with others on a table against one wall. Nancy studied the addition. It was a big square room enclosing what looked like a shallow swimming pool. Fixed in the center of the pool was the middle section of a racing shell, with eight seats for the oarsmen and one seat, facing forward, for the coxswain.

Nancy was going to ask Rob a question, but he was staring moodily down at the floor at the end of their row.

"It has recirculating pumps," Jerry was explaining to George. "It's supposed to feel as though you're rowing on a real lake or river. You can even adjust the speed of the current."

"Oops," Bess said, "I think I see some more speeches coming." She nodded toward a group that had just come in. Nancy recognized Garrison Butler, the president of Emerson College.

After welcoming the audience, President Butler turned the microphone over to the crew coach. Nancy found herself tuning out his speech, until a familiar name caught her attention.

"To Rob Harper, who went on believing in this dream when the rest of us were ready to give up. Where are you, Rob? Take a bow."

Nancy looked at the end of their row, but the chair where Rob had been sitting was empty. Where *was* he? He must have slipped away. Under the circumstances, Nancy couldn't blame him.

"I'll pass on our appreciation to Rob the next time I see him," the coach continued. "Finally, I'd like to thank one of our most steadfast supporters, a great sportsman, and one of our crew team's biggest fans, Mr. William Whorf."

As Whorf stepped forward and waved, George leaned over and whispered to Nancy, "If this guy keeps up his donations, Emerson will probably be changed to *Whorf* College before long."

Nancy chuckled but stopped when someone behind them said, *"Shh!"*

The coach was announcing that the junior varsity crew would demonstrate the new tank. As nine guys wearing sweatpants and shirts bearing the Emerson emblem clambered into the shell, Nancy sniffed the air, frowned, and looked around her. A few feet away was a door that must lead into the old part of the boat house. From under the bottom edge of the door came a few thin wisps of gray smoke. As she looked, the wisps thickened and darkened, and an acrid smell reached her nostrils.

"Fire!" someone near her shouted. *"Fire!"*

Chapter

Three

THE AUDIENCE LEAPT to their feet as frantic cries echoed back and forth in the big room. Someone a few rows over let out a single bloodcurdling scream. Someone else gave Nancy a shove that almost knocked her off her feet. Fear and panic rippled through the crowd, and Nancy knew that could be as dangerous as the fire itself. Keeping her voice steady, she began to direct people to the exit. Gradually, people calmed down a little and started toward the outside door.

"Stick together," Nancy told her friends in an urgent tone. Ned was right behind her, his arm linked with Jerry's. Bess, looking pale, took Nancy's and George's arms.

27

"Everybody, remain calm," the amplifier boomed. President Butler had grabbed the microphone. "Just proceed to the exit in an orderly fashion and everybody will be safe."

People had stopped shoving and were moving in an orderly fashion toward the open door. The members of the crew, easy to recognize in their Emerson sweats, had lined up near the door to direct traffic.

After what seemed like forever, Nancy found herself outside. Taking a deep breath, she looked around. "Where's Rob?" she asked.

"He left earlier," Bess replied. "All of a sudden he just got up and stormed away. He looked pretty upset."

Nancy quickly explained about Rob's having been suspended from the crew, then turned her attention back to the fire. Smoke was rising into the air from the older part of the building, but it looked as though it was coming from just one window. She didn't see any flames.

In the distance sirens wailed. A handful of campus police had arrived and moved the crowd farther from the building.

"Let's go around to the front of the boat house," Nancy said. "There's something about this fire that doesn't feel right to me."

"What do you mean?" demanded Jerry.

"The timing," Nancy told him. "Does it seem

like a coincidence that the fire broke out right in the middle of the dedication ceremony?"

Two fire engines roared up and stopped in front of the boat house. A pair of fire fighters dragged a hose, while others, wearing breathing masks, attacked the nearest set of doors with axes and crowbars before rushing in with foam extinguishers.

Black smoke billowed out the open doors, causing the crowd of spectators to back up. As Nancy watched, the smoke changed to gray, then to white. A few seconds later two fire fighters armed with long pikes dragged a smoldering mass out the door and threw it on the lawn before spraying it with foam.

"That was the fire?" Bess said. "What is it?"

"It looks like some kind of cloth," George said as the fire fighters used their pikes to spread out the red-hot pile. "Towels or something."

Nancy frowned. "I never heard of towels catching fire all by themselves," she remarked. She was becoming more and more positive that her suspicions about the fire were correct.

A man in a fire chief's uniform spoke to two of the fire fighters before joining President Butler.

"I'll be right back," Nancy murmured to Ned. She edged her way through the crowd until she was within hearing distance of the college president and the fire chief.

"We'll have to wait for the results of our investigation," the fire chief was saying. "But unofficially, I don't think there's any question about it. This was arson."

Nancy nodded. She had been right—someone *had* set the fire on purpose.

"That's terrible," Butler exclaimed. "We could have had a real tragedy on our hands."

"Yes, sir. Though if I'm right, I don't think the perpetrator meant to do much damage. The fire was more of a gesture. But like most people, he might not have realized that the worst danger is from smoke. We could have had a very deadly situation on our hands."

President Butler took a deep breath. "Well, thank you, Chief Culliver. I appreciate the information. You'll keep me informed?"

"Of course." The chief turned and went into the boat house.

Nancy returned to her friends. "I was right about the fire," she announced.

"You mean somebody deliberately set it?" George demanded, her dark eyes open wide. "Why would anyone do such a thing?"

"I don't know," Nancy answered. "But it seems pretty clear that whoever did it intended to disrupt the dedication ceremonies."

"It must have been some nut," Jerry put in. "You don't try to burn down a building full of people just because you got out of bed on the wrong side."

Nancy shrugged her shoulders. Suddenly she realized that she was freezing, and she rubbed her arms vigorously.

"Need this?" Ned asked, holding out her parka. "One of the fire fighters brought our jackets out while you were gone."

Nancy put on her jacket, her mind still on the fire. "Whoever set it could be somebody who has a lot of resentment against the new building, or maybe against the college as a whole. Somebody who feels unfairly treated." Somebody like Rob, she thought, but her instincts told her he wouldn't have done it. She did have to admit that he had a motive—and the opportunity.

"I can't imagine—" Bess began.

Just then Rob came running up and grabbed Ned's arm. "What happened? What's going on?" he demanded breathlessly.

"Where were you?" Ned said. "Did you miss the fire?"

Rob stared at him. "Fire? In the boat house? The shells! Were they damaged?"

Nancy watched him closely. He seemed genuinely surprised—and upset. "The fire chief says that there was hardly any damage," she assured him.

"Thank goodness!" Rob said. He took a deep

breath, then wiped his forehead. Nancy noticed he was damp with sweat in spite of the cold.

"You must be frozen," Bess said sympathetically. "Where's your jacket?"

Rob looked down at his sweater and frowned in confusion. "I guess I left it inside," he said, glancing around vaguely. "I had to get out of there, so I went for a run. I didn't think about my jacket. I guess I'd better go get it. I'll catch you guys later."

Now that the fire was obviously out, the crowd in front of the boat house began to disperse.

Jerry looked at his watch. "What now, gang? We've still got some time before lunch."

"We could put in a little more work on our snow sculptures," Nancy suggested.

"Good idea," agreed Bess. "Mine needs some serious work. Every time I think I'm getting somewhere, part of it flakes off."

"That's why they're called snowflakes," Jerry quipped, causing the others to groan.

A few people were working on their sculptures when Nancy's group returned. One of them was Susan, who was sculpting a mound that resembled a car or sled.

When Nancy called out a greeting, Susan jumped nervously. "Oh, hi," Susan said with a halfhearted smile.

"Susan," Nancy began. "I don't mean to pry or

32

anything. It's just that I don't want you to feel uneasy about our spending time with Rob. We didn't realize you two didn't get along—"

"It's no problem," Susan cut in. "I don't mean to be a drag. If you guys want to hang out with Rob Harper, it's fine with me."

As Susan bent back over her sculpture, something else caught Nancy's attention.

"Hey," she said. "Someone's been messing with my snowman." Her two huge snowballs were cracked and lopsided.

"Mine, too," Bess said. She pointed to a hunk that had been knocked loose from her snow tower. "Talk about nerve!"

"At the risk of sounding like a broken record," George added, "someone's been messing with *my* sculpture, too. I think I can fix it, though."

Nancy walked slowly around the snow-covered meadow, then returned to her friends. "It looks to me as if about half of the sculptures have been damaged," she reported.

"I wonder why?" George asked. "Accident? Thoughtlessness? Or just plain malice?"

"Maybe someone wants to win the contest, no matter what it takes," Bess suggested darkly.

Ned shook his head and chuckled. "If it meant winning a new car or a trip to Europe, I could see it. But as chief judge, I can tell you that all the winner gets is a handshake."

"Oh, well, it doesn't matter," Nancy said optimistically. "I just hope whoever did it doesn't do it again."

"Uh-oh," Ned said, cocking his head to one side. "Do you hear that? I hope our arsonist hasn't struck again."

From somewhere in the distance came the wail of sirens. "I think they're coming this way," George said.

"That's not a fire engine," Jerry reported, pointing up the hill toward the road. "It's a police car—no, make that *two* police cars."

Red lights flashing, the cars pulled up in front of the Emerson Museum. Half a dozen uniformed officers and two men in suits jumped out and ran inside.

"Come on," Nancy said, taking off across the meadow for the museum. At the road, she paused as another patrol car sped past and pulled up next to the museum. She recognized the two men who got out and hurried inside. One was President Butler. The other was Dean Jarvis, whom she had met during an earlier case at Emerson College.

"What is it?" George demanded as she, Ned, Jerry, and Bess caught up to Nancy.

"I don't know yet," Nancy replied, "but it's important enough to bring the president and the dean on the run."

The metal doors to the museum swung open just as Nancy reached the top of the hill. A police officer escorted about a half-dozen confused-looking students outside, then closed the door.

"Maybe they know what's going on," Bess said.

"They're bound to know more than we do," Ned replied. He cupped his hands to his mouth and called, "Hey, Frazier! Over here!"

A guy with bright red hair looked around, then walked over to join them.

Ned introduced Nancy, George, and Bess, then asked, "What's the story?"

"Somebody robbed the place," Frazier reported cheerfully. "They actually searched us before they'd let us leave."

"The museum? Oh, no!" exclaimed Bess.

"Did the thief get away with much?" George asked.

"Yes and no," Frazier answered. "From what I heard before they kicked us out, he just took one set of jewelry. But it's one of the most valuable sets in the whole show. A necklace, a couple of bracelets, and a pair of earrings made of diamonds and rubies. They used to belong to some queen."

Nancy gasped. The Empress of Austria's jewels had been stolen!

Chapter

Four

"OH, NO," BESS WAILED. "You mean that ruby set I loved so much is gone?"

"At least the thief had good taste," Ned put in.

Nancy frowned. "What I don't understand is how the thief got past the guards and the new alarm system."

Frazier shrugged. "We were just going through the exhibit when all of a sudden the alarm went off."

Bess's blue eyes widened. "You mean the thief struck with everyone right there in the museum?"

Frazier shook his head. "Nope. *That* was a

false alarm. Apparently it's not the first one they've had, either. But the noise was driving everyone crazy, so one of the guards turned off the system and went to check out the problem.

"Right after the false alarm, we heard the fire engines going to the boat house. Everyone ran to the windows to see what was happening."

"The guards, too?" asked George. "I bet they're going to catch a lot of grief over that."

"And *that's* when the thief struck," Nancy concluded. "While the alarm system was turned off and the exhibit was empty."

Frazier nodded. "Neat, huh?"

"But the fire happened over a half hour ago. Why did it take so long for the guards to notice the theft?" Nancy asked.

"This guy must be a real pro," Frazier cut in. "The cops said he left some costume jewelry in the display case, in place of the real stuff. I guess it took a while for anyone to notice."

The museum door opened just then, and Dean Jarvis, a bear of a man in a brown tweed suit and trench coat, came out. He paused on the steps and stared out pensively at the landscape. He wore a dissatisfied expression on his face. Then his gaze fell on Nancy and his eyes widened. He hesitated for only a moment before walking over to her and her friends.

"Hello, Dean Jarvis," Nancy said, smiling. "It's nice to see you again."

He nodded to everyone, then said, "Hello, Nancy. I'm glad to see you. You must be here for Winter Carnival."

"That's right."

"I hope you're enjoying yourself. I suppose you've heard about what just happened."

"The empress's rubies? Yes. Do the police have any leads?"

Dean Jarvis shrugged. "I'm not in their confidence, but I believe they have the matter in hand. I hope they make swift progress. The exhibition is insured, of course, but this sort of thing is not good for the image of the college."

"If I can be of any help—" Nancy said tentatively.

The dean shook his head. "Thanks, but I don't want to put you in danger a second time. This is a job for the police, and I'm sure they'll do it competently. If you'll excuse me, I have to go."

Dean Jarvis had recently asked Nancy's help in solving the theft of controlled substances from a top-secret government science experiment being done at Emerson. She appreciated his concern for her safety, but she also felt a stab of disappointment as he left. She was dying to get in on the case.

Ned noticed her reaction. "Never mind, Nancy. You don't have to solve a crime to have a good time."

She looked up at him and smiled. "Not if I'm with you, I don't." She snuggled up next to him and felt his arm wrap firmly around her shoulders.

"All the same," Nancy added, "I'm going to keep my eyes open. There are some peculiar things about this robbery. *Very* peculiar. First the boat house fire, then the theft of the empress's jewels."

"Hey, there's Rob," George said. "He must be looking for us." She walked to the edge of the bluff, called out, and waved. From down near the snow sculptures, Rob waved back and started toward the steps. Nancy noticed that he was wearing a tan parka instead of his crew jacket.

"I couldn't find my jacket at the boat house," Rob said glumly when he reached them. "Someone must have taken it by accident. I had to go all the way back to the dorm for another jacket."

"That other jacket had your name embroidered on it," George pointed out. "Anyone who took it will figure out the mistake soon enough."

"That's true." Rob's face brightened. Then he noticed the two police cars. "Hey, *now* what's happened?"

Ned told him about the jewel theft.

"You're kidding!" He looked at Bess and smiled. "I think you have some explaining to do," he teased.

"Explanations can wait until after lunch," Jerry announced. "Come on. All this excitement has given me a real appetite."

After lunch Nancy, Bess, and George returned to their room to get their ice skates, then rejoined the guys outside the dorm.

Jerry immediately began to stalk a giggling Bess with a gloveful of snow and the clear intention of putting it down the back of her neck.

George's date was paying a lot of attention to Bess, Nancy thought. "What I don't understand," Ned was saying, "is why the thief took only one set of jewelry. Why not grab as much as he could while the alarm was off?"

"For that matter, why take that set at all?" Rob said as George came up. "They were the best-known pieces in the whole show. Anyone who knows about antique jewelry would recognize it. And if the thief breaks it up for the stones, he won't get enough to make the risk worthwhile."

Bess stopped and gasped, having overheard. "You mean someone might actually destroy those beautiful works of art just to get the stones? That's terrible— *Eek!*" She spun around and brushed at her collar, trying to dislodge the snowball Jerry had just put there.

"So someone," Nancy said, "—either the thief or someone who hired the thief—must want that jewelry to keep for himself."

Ned nodded. "An unscrupulous collector," he added. "It's the only answer that makes sense."

"Unless somebody has a grudge against Emerson College and wants to hurt its reputation," said George. "If that's the motive, then who knows what he might do next?"

Nancy considered George's suggestion. She had a strong feeling that the criminal had a different motive than just revenge against the campus. The theft had been too specific for that.

"Uh-oh," said Ned, breaking into her thoughts. "I recognize that look, Drew. It's the same one you get every time you start a new case. Sorry, but any detecting will have to wait until we've gone skating. Come on. Let's get down to the lake." He grabbed Nancy's hand and started pulling her down the path.

Nancy was the first to get her skates laced. "I want to test out the ice," she said.

She pushed off and started skating toward the boat house. Behind her, she heard Ned call out something, but she couldn't make out the words. Taking a deep breath, she started to pick up speed. Skating on a lake was so different from a rink. The ice was bumpier, of course, but the frozen expanse made her feel as if she could skate forever. This was real freedom, gliding along with no effort and no limits.

Oops! About a hundred feet down the lake, someone had placed three striped sawhorses across the ice. A sign hung from the one in the middle. So much for no limits, she thought to herself. She guessed what the sign said even before she was close enough to read the words painted in red: Danger—Thin Ice.

She slid to a halt and looked around, just as Ned skated up and stopped next to her. "I wasn't sure if they'd put up the barriers," he said breathlessly, his eyes filled with concern. "There's a spring under here that keeps this section of the lake from freezing as solid as the rest. When I was a freshman, someone fell through and almost drowned."

"I'm lucky the sawhorses were there." Nancy took his gloved hand and gave it a warm squeeze. "Let's get back to the others." Still holding hands, they pushed off, falling easily into a rhythm that carried them swiftly toward the rest of the skaters.

As they drew closer, Nancy noticed Rob skating off toward the far side of the lake, in the direction of the boat house. He waved when he saw them. Nancy thought he was probably still worried about the boat house fire. She, too, had been wondering about it. She suspected the fire had been set as a decoy, so that the thief could make off with the empress's jewels. But as to *who* the thief was, she didn't have a clue.

George emerged from the little crowd of skaters and zipped over to Nancy and Ned, spraying up a small shower of ice with her stop. "This is great," she said. "It's a lot bigger than the skating pond in River Heights."

"Hey, take a look at Bess," Nancy said. "If it isn't Miss Ice Capades herself!"

George's smile broadened. "A few minutes ago she was telling Jerry about a figure-skating championship she saw on television last week. I think she's trying to demonstrate."

"I can tell you one thing," Nancy said with a laugh. "She'll never make it to the Olympics."

"Don't tell me, tell her," George said. "Oops!"

A complicated series of moves had just left Bess skating backward toward Nancy, George, and Ned. She was balancing on one leg and holding the other up behind her. Her arms, out to either side, waved and dipped comically as she wobbled unsteadily backward.

Jerry, skating parallel to her, shouted, "Terrific, Bess!"

Bess turned her head to smile at him, but that turned out to be a big mistake. A sudden dip to the left, another to the right, and Bess was sliding facedown over the ice—still moving backward.

Nancy got to her before she had even stopped sliding. "Are you okay?" she asked, trying to suppress a laugh as she helped Bess into a sitting position. "Did you hurt yourself?"

"I think I bruised my pride," Bess said, but her blue eyes were twinkling. "But so what? *I* didn't even know I could do that!"

"I'm still not so sure you can," George teased. She bent down to help her cousin to her feet. "Warn me the next time you plan to try it. I'll bring my camera."

Bess brushed herself off and straightened up. Suddenly her face became very alert. "What's that?" she said, sniffing the air. "Do I smell hot cocoa?"

"You bet," Jerry said. "I saw some guys making a big pot of it. Would you like some?"

"I think I *need* some," Bess replied with a big smile. "For medicinal purposes."

"Sounds good to me, too," Nancy added.

The group skated toward the shore, where there was a firepit and a pile of wood. A couple of guys had built a bonfire, and a pot of cocoa rested on the embers at one end.

As Nancy and the others were taking off their skates, Rob rejoined them. He rubbed his gloved hands together, then sat down and began to untie his skates. "Mmm, I can't wait for some of that cocoa." He elbowed George good-naturedly. "How about you?"

Nancy noticed a police officer standing close by. With her was a man who looked familiar to Nancy, although she couldn't quite place him. Both of them were scanning the crowd.

The man stared at Nancy and her friends. Suddenly he grabbed the officer's arm and said something into her ear. The officer stared at them, too, then she and the man began to walk toward Nancy's group. What was going on?

As they drew closer, Nancy recalled where she had seen the man before. He was the museum guard who had been in the room with the Empress of Austria's jewels.

"That's him," she heard the guard say to the officer. "I'm sure of it."

The officer stepped over to Rob and said, "Excuse me, sir. Would you mind telling me your name?"

Rob looked up from unlacing his skates. "Me? Robert Harper. Why?"

The officer said, "I'd like you to come with me, please, when you've finished with your skates."

Rob looked baffled. "Come with you where? Why?"

The officer looked at him and replied, "To the police station. We just want to ask you some questions. But I think it's fair to warn you that you might be a suspect in the Emerson Museum jewelry theft!"

Chapter

Five

NANCY WATCHED with growing concern as the police car took Rob away. Once it was out of sight, everyone standing near the bonfire began to talk at once in subdued voices.

"Why on earth do they want to question Rob?" George muttered to Nancy.

"The guard singled him out," Nancy answered. "Remember last night in the museum, the way Rob boasted that he could get around the alarm system? And the way he and Bess kept leaning over the case with the jewels that were stolen this morning? Their fingerprints are probably all over that display case."

"But that's not evidence," George protested.

"Dozens of people must have touched that case!"

"I know," Nancy said. "But don't forget that one of them was probably the thief. It's their responsibility to check out everyone who's the least bit suspicious."

Bess had been talking to Jerry, her mug of hot cocoa in one hand and a stick with a toasted marshmallow on it in the other. Now she turned to Nancy and said, "We've got to do something about this. We've got to find out who really stole the jewels." Before popping the gooey marshmallow into her mouth, she added, "And if I know you, you've already got some suspects."

"I have a couple," Nancy told them. "But I'm going to need a lot of help."

"Just tell us what to do," Jerry volunteered, with a snappy salute that made Bess giggle.

Nancy took a few steps away from the crowd, and Bess, George, Ned, and Jerry followed her. "I'd like you all to talk to people who either visited the museum or attended the boat house dedication this morning."

"What are we looking for?" asked George.

Nancy grimaced. "I don't know, exactly," she confessed. "Find out who they saw and talked to. Beyond that, look for anything out of the ordinary."

"You think the fire at the boat house was linked to the robbery?" Jerry asked.

"The timing was just too neat to be a coincidence," Nancy said, glancing at her watch. "We should get on with it. What do you say we meet in the student center in an hour?"

"What are you going to do now?" Ned asked her as the others walked away. "Can I help?"

Nancy shook her head. "I'm going to try to get permission from the college authorities to solve the theft," she said. "They can't stop me, in any event, but it would make my work easier if they cooperated."

Nancy skipped up the stairs that led to the main part of the campus. She felt lighter since George had offered to take her skates back to the dorm. Before heading over to the administration building, however, she decided to stop at the Emerson Museum. Luck was with her. Dean Jarvis's car was still parked in front. She climbed the steps and banged on the closed doors. No response. She looked around and finding a small bell to one side, she pressed it. Half a minute later, the door opened a couple of inches and the guard who had identified Rob looked out at her.

"Sorry, the museum's closed for the day," he said gruffly, starting to close the door.

"I'd like to speak to Dean Jarvis," Nancy said

quickly. "I believe he's inside. Please tell him it's Nancy Drew."

The guard scowled. "I don't—" he began.

"It's very important," Nancy pressed.

"Okay, hold on." After a few moments the door opened and the guard reappeared. "Okay," he told her, "come on in. Dean Jarvis is over there."

Dean Jarvis was standing with President Butler and Mr. Whorf. All three men glanced over at Nancy as she started across the entrance hall.

Dean Jarvis stepped away from the others and met her in the middle of the hall. "What is it, Nancy?" he asked in a low voice. "The guard said it was important."

"It's about the jewel theft," Nancy said. "Have you heard that the police have taken one of your students, Rob Harper, down to the station for questioning?"

Jarvis drew his eyebrows together. "Harper? No, I—I know they've been questioning a few people here," he continued. "I didn't know they had taken anyone to the station."

"I don't think Rob had anything to do with the theft," Nancy said, "but I don't have proof at this point. What I would like from you is the college's permission to look into the case."

"Harper is a friend of Ned Nickerson, isn't he?"

Nancy felt her cheeks redden. "Yes," she said. "He is. But I can give you my word that won't affect the way I handle the case. If I find evidence that Rob *was* involved, I'll turn it over to the authorities immediately."

Jarvis looked embarrassed. "I didn't mean to suggest that you wouldn't," he said quickly. "I was thinking more of how it might look to someone who doesn't know you—the police, for instance."

He rubbed his temples while he thought. At last he said, "All right, Nancy, you have my permission to investigate. You've helped the college out of tight spots before, and we can certainly use your help now."

"Thanks, Dean," Nancy said, smiling. "Would you mind if I check a couple of things with you? Is it definite that the jewels were stolen while the guards were distracted by the fire at the boat house?"

"Oh, yes."

"How many people were in the museum at the time of the theft?" Nancy asked.

"About a dozen, from what I've heard," Jarvis replied. "Plus the two guards. But once they heard the sirens, they all left the exhibit area and went to see what was going on. The police couldn't find anyone who didn't, as a matter of fact."

51

"So the exhibit was empty—except for the thief," Nancy pointed out. "Okay, thanks, Dean. I'd better get to work."

"Thank *you*, Nancy," he said. "And good luck."

Nancy went slowly through the museum, checking out its layout and looking for anything unusual. As she expected, the emergency exit was just outside the last room of the jewelry exhibit —the room where the empress's jewels had been displayed. The security room, where the alarm system was located, was a small, cramped room at the very back of the museum, far from both the exhibit and the entrance to the museum.

After finishing her inspection, she asked the guards a few questions, then checked her watch. She still had time before she had to meet the others at the student center, so she sat down on a bench in the museum's entrance hall to think.

The thief had probably used the emergency entrance to make his exit. Since the alarm had already been shut off, there was no fear of it sounding. But how had he gotten in without anyone seeing him? She wished she could get a copy of the list of people who'd been in the museum at the time, but that didn't seem possible.

Sighing, Nancy propped her elbows on her jeans and rested her chin in the palms of her hands. There was the question of how the boat house fire fit in, too. If the same person was responsible for both crimes, as she suspected, then he or she would have had to make quick time getting from the boat house to the museum after setting the fire. How long a walk was it?

There were two ways to go: along the lakeshore and past the field with the snow sculptures to the steps leading up the hill, or along the path that led through the little wood and up a gentler slope farther down the hill. The lake path seemed as if it might be a bit more direct, but it was also much more exposed. Nancy had a hunch that the thief would have taken the more hidden path instead.

Zipping up her jacket, she braced herself for the cold and headed along the bluff in the direction of the path that would lead to the small woods. The stretch of road between the museum and the path was pretty deserted—there weren't any buildings, and there was a good cover of evergreens on both sides.

Nancy turned down the path. She kept a sharp lookout for anything unusual, pausing every so often to glance into the woods on either side of the path. She was about halfway through the woods when she noticed a line of footprints that left the path to enter a small clump of evergreens. Another line of footprints returned to the path a few yards farther on. The prints looked fresh, their edges still sharp. She bent down to peer in under the trees and felt her heart start to beat faster. What was that dark shape on the snow?

Carefully avoiding the two lines of footprints, she made her way across the snow and ducked under the interlaced branches. As she neared the shadowy objects, the strong smell of gasoline filled the air.

Nancy then saw that the shadow was a purple jacket with orange leather sleeves lying crumpled up on the snow. Jackpot! she thought triumphantly. Maybe the jacket belonged to whoever had set the boat house fire? When she bent down to pick it up, the harsh odor of gasoline intensified, causing her to cough.

She carried the jacket back out to the path and held it up. She gasped when she saw the crossed oars on the back. There was a sinking feeling in her stomach as she turned the jacket around to read the name embroidered on the front.

The jacket belonged to Rob Harper!

Chapter

Six

As Nancy stared at the jacket, a whiff of gasoline burned her nose, sending her into another coughing fit. But before she could get her breath back, a hand suddenly grabbed her shoulder.

"Okay, young lady," a gruff voice said. "You'd better hand that over and explain what you're doing!"

Nancy whirled around and found herself face-to-face with a beefy police officer, who sported a crew cut and glasses. She'd been coughing so hard she hadn't heard him come up behind her.

"Officer, I think I've just found—"

"You're coming with me, miss," the officer cut in. "You've got a lot of explaining to do!"

If you'll let me, Nancy said to herself.

Forty-five minutes later, at the police station, Nancy was still trying to explain what had happened, but no one was listening.

"Look, Sergeant Balsam," she said for what seemed like the billionth time, "if you'll just telephone Dean Jarvis—"

"I'll get to that, Ms. Drew," the police sergeant said. "But first," he continued, "I'd like you to tell me again what you were doing in those woods with that jacket."

"I already—" Nancy began.

He cut her off. "I know, you already told me. But I have a short memory, especially when I'm talking to people who've been tampering with important evidence. Try telling me again."

Nancy sighed and shifted in her chair. "I was walking along the path from the museum to the boat house," she said wearily, "when I noticed some footprints going off into a clump of trees. Then I saw something lying on the ground in the middle of the trees. It was the jacket. When I brought it out to the path where the light was better, your officer came along."

"Uh-huh," the sergeant said. He frowned at her. "What would you say if I told you that a police team swept that area earlier today and didn't find a jacket or anything else? Would that make you think again about your story?"

"I'm sorry, Sergeant," Nancy said firmly. "I've just told you what happened. Either your crew missed the jacket earlier or it wasn't put there until later."

"You wouldn't have been in the process of putting it there yourself, would you?"

Nancy reminded herself to be patient and polite. "If you would just call Dean Jarvis," she repeated, "he'll tell you who I am."

"A detective," Sergeant Balsam said with disdain. "Is that right? An *amateur* detective. And you think you're going to make fools of the police by solving this theft when we can't. Is that right, Ms. Drew?"

"No, of course not, Sergeant. But sometimes I can find out things that the police can't—*because* I'm an amateur." Somehow, she didn't think the sergeant would appreciate hearing that.

"Uh-huh." The sergeant straightened up and adjusted his gun belt. "Would you mind telling me where you were at the time the fire in the boat house was discovered?"

"Not at all. I was at the dedication ceremony for the new rowing tank. I was standing with four friends, all of whom can vouch for me. I'll be glad to give you their names if you like."

"Later, maybe. And what did you do at that point?"

Nancy thought back, then replied, "We went around to the front of the boat house to watch the fire fighters."

"Together?"

"Together," Nancy replied with a nod.

"And was Rob Harper part of your group?"

Nancy hesitated for a moment. She didn't want to make things worse for Rob than they already were, but she couldn't lie to the police. She just hoped he wasn't counting on his friends to give him an alibi.

"He was with us when the ceremony started," Nancy said, choosing her words with care. "I don't recall seeing him when the fire was discovered. There was a lot of confusion."

"So I hear," the sergeant said. "But he rejoined you while you were standing in front of the boat house. Is that right?"

"That's right," Nancy said.

"At that time, was he wearing this jacket?" Sergeant Balsam pointed to the purple and orange jacket.

"No, just a sweater," Nancy replied, with a sinking feeling. The evidence was all too neatly pointing at Rob.

"I see." The sergeant walked over to his desk and picked up the telephone. Keeping his back to

Nancy, he dialed and spoke in a low voice to the person who answered. When he hung up, he said, "All right, Ms. Drew. I just spoke to Dean Jarvis. You can go. But let me give you a piece of advice. Don't interfere with our investigation. You'll just muddy the water for us, and that can make us feel real angry."

"Thank you, Sergeant Balsam," Nancy replied. As she stood up, she added, "What about Rob? Is he free to leave?"

Without answering Nancy's question, the sergeant walked out of the room. A few moments later he returned with Rob.

"Nancy!" Rob exclaimed. "What are you doing here?"

"That's a long story," Nancy told him. She looked at the sergeant. "May we go now?"

"Yes," he said gruffly. Shooting Rob a wary glance, he added, "But don't think you've heard the last of this."

"Let's go," Nancy said to Rob. "The others are probably worried about us."

As they walked back to the campus, Rob told her about the questions the police had asked him. "I can't believe they think I set that fire. I mean, crewing is the most important thing I do at Emerson," he said, shaking his head. "I would never sabotage the boat house!"

Nancy gave him a sympathetic look. She believed him, but considering the evidence so far—the jacket, his disappearance during the dedication ceremony, and his being suspended from the crew team—it would be tough to prove his innocence.

"Look, Rob," she said, "where exactly did you go when you left the dedication ceremony? It's important for you to establish an alibi. Everybody knows you weren't at the ceremony, because the coach thanked you by name and asked you to stand up."

"He did?" Rob asked, surprised. "I didn't know that. I'm glad I had the sense to duck out. I don't know if I could have stood that, after everything that's happened."

He took a deep breath before continuing.

"I was feeling so . . . I don't know, restless and upset about being off the team that I decided to go for a run across campus to Foster Gate, then back the long way by the heating plant."

Nancy nodded. "Did you see anybody you know?"

"The cops asked me that, too," he said. "And I'll tell you what I told them. I didn't notice anybody. I'm not saying I didn't pass a few people, but I didn't pay any attention."

Nancy sighed. If nobody saw him, it would be impossible to find someone who could verify his story. Rob sure wasn't making her job any easier. "What about your jacket? Are you sure you left it in the boat house?"

"I'm positive!" he shouted. "I'm sorry. It's just that I've done nothing for the last half hour except answer questions about that stupid jacket."

"Do you have any idea how it could have gotten soaked with gasoline?"

He raised his hands, palms up, in a gesture of exasperation. "How should I know?" he said miserably. "I don't understand any of this. I mean, when I woke up this morning I was just a normal student like everyone else. Now all of a sudden I'm a major criminal!" He shook his head. "Do you realize that on top of setting the boat house fire, the cops think I stole those jewels? Can you believe it?"

"I can't believe you did it," Nancy admitted. "But you'd better face the fact that the police have good reason to suspect you. And it looks as if somebody is trying to give them better reasons."

Rob looked at her in disbelief. "You mean someone's setting me up?"

Nancy nodded. "It looks that way. Can you think of anybody who might want to get you in trouble?"

"Not this kind of trouble," he said. "I'm not saying everybody's a friend of mine, but I usually get along with people."

Nancy studied Rob's face. His expression was sincere. "Okay," she said reassuringly. "But if anything comes to mind, let me know."

Another twenty minutes brought them to the student center. As they walked in the door, Ned called out, "Nancy! Rob!" and rushed over to them. "I was so worried. What happened to you?" he asked, taking Nancy's hand in his. "We thought you'd get here an hour ago! We were just about to go look for you."

"I might as well tell everyone at the same time," Nancy said, leading Ned over to the others.

While Nancy told them about finding Rob's jacket and being taken in for questioning by the police, Rob stood by silently, a gloomy expression on his face.

Jerry turned to him, clapped him on the shoulder, and said, "Ol' buddy, it sounds to me like somebody is fitting you for a frame."

"I already told Nancy, nobody dislikes me that much," Rob said in a downcast voice.

"But maybe somebody simply wants to send the police off on a false trail. Maybe the reason you're the target is that the thief happened to find your jacket and realized that he could use it."

"You mean the thief might not have any connection at all to Rob?" Bess said. "Then how on earth are we ever going to track him down?"

"The usual mixture," Nancy said. "Sound thinking, hard work, and a touch of good luck."

"I sure could use the good luck," Rob said, smiling weakly. "But let's not talk about my problems anymore. It's Winter Carnival, after all."

Nancy was glad he was making an effort to cheer up, even if it was only for everyone else's sake. Glancing over Rob's shoulder, Nancy saw someone who wouldn't help his mood.

Rob was unzipping his parka and starting to take it off just as Susan Samuels walked past. She ducked to dodge his outstretched arm, but ended up falling against him. She tumbled to the stone floor.

"Sorry," Susan and Rob said at the same instant. As he reached down to help her to her feet, she looked up and recognized him.

"Get your hands off me!" Susan said, pushing him away.

"I'm sorry, I didn't mean—" Rob began.

"You heard her, Harper," a deep voice said.

Nancy turned to see a guy who was half a foot shorter than Rob, but just as wide and muscular. He was wearing a motorcycle jacket and a long wool muffler in the Emerson colors of purple and orange. He grabbed the collar of Rob's parka and added, "Back off!"

Rob pushed the guy's hand away and said, "Get lost, Forsyte. What makes you think you can give me orders?"

For an answer, the other guy planted his feet solidly on the floor and drew back his arm to throw a punch at Rob's face!

Chapter

Seven

GREG, NO!" Susan screamed.

Rob's hands tightened into fists, and the look on his face told Nancy that he would welcome a good reason to strike out at anyone. Grabbing his arm, she said, "Rob, don't."

At the same time, Ned and Jerry moved in between Rob and the guy Susan had called Greg. "Hey, cut it out, you guys," Ned shouted.

He took Rob by the shoulders and urged him to back up, while Jerry stood right in front of Greg, talking to him in a low, calm voice.

"I want him to stay away from Susan," Greg said loudly.

"You get no argument from me on that, fella," Rob replied.

"There," Jerry said. "He'll stay away from Susan. Okay?"

Greg's face was still red, his fists still clenched. "I don't like the way you said that," he muttered, glaring at Rob.

Jerry put a hand on each of Greg's shoulders. "Nobody wants any trouble," he said. "So why don't we all just go our own ways?"

Greg scowled up at Jerry. "I don't like—"

Susan took his arm. "Come on, Greg," she said. "Let's just drop it."

"Drop it?" he said. "That guy almost knocked you down. You want to let him get away with that?"

"It was an accident," Susan told him. "He wasn't paying attention, and I wasn't looking where I was going. That's all."

"You deserve an apology," Greg insisted, glaring around Jerry's arm at Rob.

Rob looked tired of the whole argument. "Hey," he said, "if it'll make any difference, I'll apologize. Okay? Susan, I'm sorry. I didn't mean to knock you down."

"There," Jerry said, urging Greg toward the door of the student center. "It's all settled now."

Susan gave Nancy an apologetic look, then followed Greg out the door.

"Well!" Bess exclaimed. "What was that all about?"

Rob looked embarrassed. "Greg tried out for the number-five oar on the varsity crew last fall. I was the number-three oar in the same boat. Well, when he found out he didn't make the cut, he said it was my fault, that I'd deliberately thrown him off his stroke."

"And had you?" Nancy asked.

Rob's face reddened. "Of course not! He just didn't have what it takes, and the coach saw it. But Greg would rather blame me than face up to that fact."

"Some facts are hard to face," Nancy observed. "But just now he seemed more concerned about Susan than his position on the crew. Why is that?"

The red in Rob's cheeks deepened. "Oh, Susan and I used to be a couple, that's all."

"That's *all?*" George repeated.

"All right, it was more than that. We dated for most of a year. We even talked about getting engaged. And then—I don't know—it just ended. We weren't having fun anymore."

"So you both agreed to break up?" Nancy asked. "No hard feelings, as they say?"

"Well . . . I'm the one who broke it off. And Susan swore she'd never forgive me. It hurt her pride that *I* broke up with *her.*"

Nancy nodded. That explained why Susan was so mad at him. "When was all this?" Nancy asked. "The breakup, I mean?"

"Oh, not long after school started."

"And you and Susan have had nothing to do with each other since?"

"A few dirty looks—from her, not from me. I'm sorry she's still mad. Maybe that's why she started going with someone who has it in for me.

"Listen," he added, "I need to go pick up some books at the library. Coach says if I can bring my marks up by midterm, he'll go to bat for me with the dean and try to get my probation lifted."

"What if your marks don't improve?" Nancy asked. "What happens then?"

Rob shrugged. "Then I'm off the crew, and the coach has to bring someone up from the JV team to take my oar. But I'm not going to let that happen. I'll see you guys later."

As Ned walked with him to the door, Nancy thought about all that had just happened. It seemed as if Greg had a motive to set Rob up. But did he have a motive for the jewelry theft? She drew a blank. She simply needed more to go on. She'd already interviewed one of the guards, but—

Then it came to her. What about the renowned William Whorf? He was involved with both the museum *and* the crew team. Maybe he'd be able to provide her with some valuable information. She'd have to try to talk with him the next day.

When Ned came back, he said, "Rob says he'll join us for dinner tonight. Jerry reserved a table at La Fleur-de-Lis."

"Ooh-la-la," Bess joked. "It sounds *très* elegant."

"It is," Jerry said. "The food's good, too."

Nancy's mind was still on the case. "Look," she said. "Is there someplace private we can sit down for a few minutes? I need to hear what you learned from talking to people."

Ned led them to a small side room furnished with a couch and a few armchairs.

"Okay," Nancy said. "Who wants to go first?"

George sat down on the arm of the couch and cleared her throat. "I had some good luck," she said. "I managed to strike up a conversation with a fire fighter who came back to take pictures of the boat house. He told me that the only thing burning when they broke in was that big pile of towels."

"Just what we thought," Nancy said.

"Uh-huh. And he said it looked as if the towels were wet. That's why there was so much smoke."

Ned shook his head. "But why would anyone set fire to wet towels?"

"For that matter," Jerry put in, "how would anyone set fire to wet towels? I'd think the dampness would put the fire out."

"I don't know how," George said, "but the fire fighter said it looked as if the fire had been set by somebody who wanted to make sure it didn't get too big. The wet towels were supposed to keep it in check."

Jerry laughed. "You mean we're looking for an arsonist who's shy and retiring?"

"No, I think we're looking for a jewel thief who turned to arson only as a needed diversion," Nancy said. "He didn't say anything about gasoline, did he?"

"Nope, not a word. Why? Oh, of course— Rob's jacket. You really don't think—"

"No," Nancy said quickly. "I don't think Rob set the fire. Someone used that jacket to try to frame him. But who? The arsonist, who is probably also the jewel thief? Or someone else? If gasoline wasn't used in the boat house fire, then it means that whoever is framing Rob is someone else who is simply trying to get him in trouble. But if it *was* used, it tells us that the framer and the arsonist are the same person, or at least that they're working together."

"Caution, detective at work," Jerry teased. Bess nudged him with her elbow, and he added, "Sorry, Nancy. I didn't mean to interrupt."

Nancy smiled. "That's okay, Jerry. I was just about to get to you. What did you find out?"

"Not very much, I'm afraid. Bess and I talked to a lot of people—"

Bess cut in. "I felt nervous about starting conversations with people I didn't know, so I asked Jerry if we could team up."

Nancy raised an eyebrow. Bess, shy? More likely, Bess had just said that so she could spend more time with Jerry.

"Right," Jerry continued. "We did talk to one girl I know who was on her way to the rowing tank dedication when she saw Rob leaving the boat house."

"The boat house?" Nancy asked. "Or the new annex where the tank is?" If he had been at the main boat house, it was likely that Rob *was* responsible for the fire.

"Oh, sorry, I meant the annex," Jerry said.

Nancy nodded, relieved. "Okay. Did your friend see what he did, or where he went?"

"She says he stood outside the door for maybe a minute, then started jogging up the road, toward this part of campus."

"And when was this, compared to the fire in the boat house?" Nancy asked.

"About five minutes before. She wasn't exactly sure, but she knows she went inside just as the coach was starting to speak."

Nancy thought back to the dedication ceremony. "I'd agree with five minutes," she said. "And that means—"

"Nancy," Ned said in a warning tone of voice. He nodded in the direction of the door.

Nancy looked around. Sergeant Balsam was standing just outside the door, looking at their faces as if committing each one to memory.

"Ms. Drew," he said, "can you tell me where to find Rob Harper?"

"Why, Sergeant?" Nancy asked. "We left the station less than an hour ago. Is there some new evidence?"

Balsam hesitated before saying, "I got a call from the fire marshal. That fire this morning was definitely arson. Tests established the presence of an accelerant."

"An accelerant?" Nancy said. "You mean—"

"I mean gasoline," Sergeant Balsam cut in. "The same kind of gasoline that was on that jacket you found. So now I have some more questions to ask Mr. Robert Harper, and this time he had better have some very good answers!"

Chapter

Eight

Rob left here a few minutes ago, Sergeant," Nancy said. "He told us he was going over to the library."

Sergeant Balsam nodded. "The library, huh? During Winter Carnival? I didn't figure him to be such a bookworm. Well, let's hope I can find him there. It hurts my feelings whenever I get the idea that somebody I'm looking for might be trying to avoid me."

"But he doesn't even know you're looking for him," George protested.

"He will," the sergeant said. "He will."

He turned and left the room. Nancy hesitated

only for a moment before getting up and following him. Somehow, she had to find a way to show him the holes in his theory that Rob set the fire.

She caught up with him just inside the student center doors. "Sergeant," she began, "can you spare me just one minute?"

"I've had a long day, Ms. Drew." He glanced at his watch. "Okay, one minute. What is it?"

Taking a deep breath, she began, "Rob's jacket. Do you have any idea how much gasoline was spilled on it? A lot. I could tell that because the fumes made me choke. Have you stopped to wonder how somebody could spill that much gasoline on his jacket and not get a drop on his pants or shoes? Because I'm ready to testify that Rob did *not* smell of gasoline when he joined us outside the boat house. And the jacket still stank of it hours later, when I found it."

The sergeant pushed his glasses up on his nose in a nervous gesture. "Sometimes there's no explaining what a perpetrator might do," he replied, but he didn't sound as convinced as he had before. "Anyway, your minute's up, unless you want to walk with me to the library."

"All right," Nancy said, running to snatch her coat, then following him out the door. "Doesn't it seem odd to you that none of your officers spotted the jacket when they went through the woods earlier?" she went on, zipping up her parka. *"I* didn't have any trouble noticing it. And now that I think about it, I'm pretty sure I smelled the gasoline, even from the path. I can't believe your officers' noses are worse than mine."

"Get to the point," the police sergeant said.

"Somebody must have poured gasoline on the jacket and put it in the middle of those trees at some point this afternoon," Nancy said. "It may have been the arsonist. But as far as I can tell, it could have been anybody—anybody who wanted to cause Rob some trouble."

"Provided they knew what was going to happen," Sergeant Balsam said.

Nancy shook her head. "Practically everybody on campus knew about it," she pointed out. "Anyway, what I'm trying to convince you of is that someone is trying to frame Rob—someone who knew he wouldn't have an alibi for the fire or the jewel theft because he had seen him leave the dedication ceremony. Probably someone inside the building, because that's where Rob must have left his jacket."

Sergeant Balsam shook his head. "Unless he spilled gas on it while he was setting up his little arson attempt," he maintained. "And I've heard he was kicked off the crew team for bad grades. Maybe he felt bitter and wanted to get revenge."

"The reason he's at the library right now is to try to bring up his grades and get his academic probation lifted so he can get back on the crew team. The last thing he'd want to do is jeopardize that."

The sergeant still looked dubious, but Nancy could tell that her arguments had at least made him doubt his iron-clad conviction that Rob was guilty. Finally he said, "I've still got every reason to question Harper. But I'll tell you what I'll do, Ms. Drew. If I find him in the library, I'll question him there instead of taking him in."

His attitude remained gruff, but Nancy realized that this was a big concession. "Thank you, Sergeant," she said.

"No thanks needed. I'm just doing my job the best I know how," he said. "And don't forget, Ms. Drew, it is *my* job. Everything I said about interference from amateurs still goes."

Nancy had no intention of dropping the case. But past experience had taught her that it was best to cooperate with the police. "I understand," she said diplomatically.

Then the sergeant turned and walked quickly toward the library.

"Nancy!" Nancy turned to see Bess standing in the doorway of the student center, propping the door open. "You're okay!"

"Of course I'm okay," she told Bess. "Why shouldn't I be?"

"Well, you were gone so long, we thought that

maybe that policeman had decided to arrest you and Rob both.''

"Hey, it's getting dark," Ned said. "We'd better go back to the dorm to change. Let's meet in the downstairs lounge of the dorm in forty-five minutes to go to the restaurant." He came down the steps and put his arm around Nancy's shoulders.

"Are you starting to feel neglected?" Nancy asked him. "This case is eating up a lot of time that we could be spending together."

"You're doing a big favor for a friend of mine and for my college," Ned pointed out. "Besides, we have this evening to have fun."

He bent his head down and kissed Nancy so sweetly that she couldn't catch her breath. When the kiss finally ended, she rested her cheek against his chest, and Ned began to stroke her hair. They might have stayed like that until both of them had frostbite, but Jerry came over and tapped Ned on the shoulder.

"Come on, Nickerson," he said. "The Fleur-de-Lis is going to be packed tonight. They won't hold our table forever."

Ned and Jerry headed for their frat house, while the girls took the path to the dorm. They were halfway there when Nancy suddenly stopped.

"Bess, George, you go ahead. There's something I want to check out." She took the room key from her pocket and handed it to George.

George opened her mouth to argue, but Bess took her arm and walked her away. "You know it won't do any good to try to talk her out of it. Please make it fast, Nan," Bess called over her shoulder. "We don't want to be late for dinner."

Nancy made her way to the path that led through the woods where she'd found Rob's jacket. As she walked, she mentally checked over her assumptions. Whoever was trying to frame Rob—whether or not it was the thief—would not have walked around with a gasoline-soaked jacket. So the jacket, and maybe the gas as well, must have been hidden for part of the afternoon, probably somewhere near the little woods where the jacket was later placed. If she could find that hiding place, she might find a clue to the identity of the framer.

She stopped in her tracks. What about the police search? They had been looking for stolen jewels, true, but wouldn't they have seen the jacket and a gasoline container?

But then, what if the police *had* seen them but hadn't noticed them? What if the jacket and the gas container had been someplace where they looked as if they belonged?

Nancy continued down the narrow road, scanning both sides in the waning, late-afternoon light. She was just up the road from the edge of the woods when she saw it. Just off the narrow lane, behind a screen of bushes, was a small wooden shed with double doors.

Nancy found her penlight in her pocket and shone it on the building. Over the doors was a small sign that read Emerson College B & G— Keep Out. Nancy nodded. "B & G" was probably an abbreviation for Buildings and Grounds, the college maintenance department. And who would be surprised to find gasoline, or even an old jacket, in a maintenance shed?

She shifted the light, then frowned. The double doors were padlocked. That meant that whoever had hidden, then retrieved, Rob's jacket from the shed had to have known the combination.

Suddenly Nancy stopped. She raised her head, standing very still, listening carefully. Had that been the sound of someone stepping on snow? She heard nothing now but the wind through the branches of some trees. Nancy looked around, but it was too dark to see anything except the outline of nearby bushes.

She stepped forward to get a closer look at the doors. The padlock was firmly fastened, but when she tugged at it, the hasp came off the door. The wood was too rotten to hold the screws.

The door creaked as Nancy pushed it open and shone her penlight inside. The shelves that lined the walls were piled high with old paint cans, broken machinery, and cardboard cartons. Two snowblowers and a riding lawnmower occupied the center of the shed.

Wishing she had a more powerful flashlight with her, Nancy began to search the shed. Just behind the mower, she found what she was looking for—a simple rectangular metal container painted red. She knelt down, taking care not to touch the can, and sniffed. The odor of gasoline was still strong.

Nancy was willing to bet that can of gasoline had been used to drench Rob's coat. Also, his jacket could have been bunched up and hidden in the shed without arousing any suspicion.

Nancy's penlight flashed on something white lying on the ground next to the gas can. She moved her light closer to the object. It was a scrap of paper—torn but crisp and white. It had some typing on it. It looked somehow familiar, but where— Nancy picked up the paper to read it.

She realized instantly what it was—a piece of the museum label from the stolen jewels!

Chapter

Nine

Nancy stared at the label. What luck! This was exactly the clue she needed. Since the museum tag was in the same place as the gasoline, that meant that the same person was probably responsible for both crimes *and* for setting up Rob.

Just then the shed door was pulled shut!

Nancy's first impulse was to run over to the door and try to force it open. But instead she made herself stand still and listen. She couldn't be positive, but she thought she heard someone running up the lane.

Nancy tucked the museum label in her pocket, then moved over to the door and pulled on it. As she had expected, it was locked tight. She pulled harder, but still it didn't budge. She thought of yelling for help but didn't think that it would do any good. The shed was pretty isolated, and she doubted that many people would be strolling down to the boat house on a winter evening.

She shone her penlight around the shed again. No windows. Now she had to find some tools to force the door open. Her penlight revealed a battered metal toolbox on a shelf. Before Nancy checked it out, she paused to think. Where were the hinges? On the inside or the outside? They had to be on the inside because the door opened *into* the shed. That meant she could remove the pins in the hinges and walk out.

She shone her light on the doorframe. The hinges were there, worn and rusty. If Nancy could slip out the pins, she'd be free.

Going over to the right-hand door, she tugged at the pin of the upper hinge. To her surprise, it slid free easily. The pin on the bottom hinge, however, was more stubborn. She pulled and pulled, but it refused to budge. Finally she took a hammer from the toolbox. Banging hard, she managed to force the second pin up and out of the hinge.

She stood up, took a deep breath, and then pushed at the edge of the right door. For one frustrating moment it didn't move. Then, with a loud screech, it swung out just enough for Nancy to squeeze through.

The chilly evening air felt wonderful in her lungs after the stale, gasoline smell of the shed. She took out her penlight and shone the small beam of light in front of the shed. A short length of lumber was jammed through the handles of the two doors.

The person who followed her had tried to trap her inside the shed.

Nancy took a last look at the shed, and her penlight shone on a tiny flash of color. She bent down to look. Caught in the edge of the door was a piece of bright orange yarn. She tucked the yarn into her pocket along with the scrap of paper.

Nancy zipped the pocket closed. She shone her light on her watch and gasped. In less than twenty minutes she was supposed to meet the others. She took off at a fast jog up the lane toward the dorm.

As she entered the dorm, Nancy passed a bank of telephone booths. She made a quick decision to call Sergeant Balsam and tell him about the gas can and the label. Despite his negative attitude toward amateur detectives, she still felt that it was important to cooperate with the police.

"What is it, Ms. Drew?" the sergeant asked brusquely.

"I think I found where the gasoline came from

and why your searchers missed that jacket earlier," she said. She told him what she had found in the shed.

"My officers spotted that gas can this afternoon," he replied, sounding bored. "It belongs there. No reason to think it has any connection with the arson attempt."

Nancy sighed with frustration. "Did they check how much gasoline was in it? Because I'll bet that a lot of it was poured over the jacket."

"Pure guesswork, Ms. Drew," the sergeant replied. "That's one thing people who read detective stories don't understand. Real police work is mostly spadework, not guesswork."

"Does that mean that they *didn't* check the level of gas in the can?" she asked.

"I'm sure they didn't touch it," he said. "Just a minute, I'll check the report. . . . Yeah, they spotted it on the shelf and left it there."

"But, Sergeant," Nancy persisted. "When I found it, it was on the ground. Don't you see? Somebody must have moved it!"

Sergeant Balsam sighed loudly into the receiver. "Okay, Ms. Drew," he said. "I'll send someone around tomorrow morning to take a look."

His tone made it clear that he was humoring her. Why wouldn't he take her seriously? "What about the museum label?" she asked.

"Well, Ms. Drew, when my officer comes

around tomorrow, you give him your piece of paper, too, and we'll see if it really is what you say. Any old piece of paper can look a lot like a label."

Nancy decided there was no point telling him about being shut in the shed—or about the yarn. He would probably think that she was making up the whole episode.

"All right, Sergeant Balsam," she said. "Thanks for your help." To herself, she added, Thanks for nothing!

When Nancy left the phone booth, she ran into Bess and George, who were already dressed and waiting in the entrance area of the dorm.

"Nancy! What took you so long?" Bess exclaimed.

"Here's the key," said George, handing it to her. "You'd better hurry, though. The guys will be here any second."

"Tell me about it," Nancy said, rushing past them. "I'll explain everything after I'm dressed," she called over her shoulder.

When Nancy got upstairs, she found Susan sitting at her desk, writing a letter. Seeing Nancy, she smiled and said, "Hi. Did you see Bess and George? They just left a minute ago."

Nancy nodded. "They're waiting for me. I have to make the fastest change in history!"

Susan laughed, her chin-length hair bouncing

around her face. "How are you liking Winter Carnival so far?" she asked.

"Well, it certainly hasn't been dull," Nancy said.

"No, I guess not! First the fire at the boat house, then the museum robbery. You can bet Emerson will make the front page of all the major newspapers. Some of us who work at the museum were wondering if it was all part of a publicity stunt."

Nancy looked at her in surprise. "You're not serious, are you?"

"No, of course not," Susan said, shaking her head. "The last thing a museum wants is to have people think its security is weak. Who'd lend it things to display? But I'm predicting crowds tomorrow, just the same."

Nancy crossed to the closet and took out the dress she was planning to wear to dinner. It was a scoop-necked minidress in rich red silk with a red flowered pattern in it.

"I love that dress," Susan said as Nancy slipped it on. "The color is great with your hair."

"Thanks." Nancy found the bracelet that Ned had given her for her birthday and clasped it on her right wrist. "Oh, Susan," she said, "I almost forgot to warn you. I'm planning to get up very early tomorrow morning. Ned and I have a skating date before breakfast. I'll do my best not to disturb you, but my travel alarm is pretty loud."

"No problem," Susan said. "I'm an early riser myself. Will you be gone all evening?"

"I'm not sure," Nancy said, grabbing her coat. "We're going out to dinner, but I don't know what's on after that."

Nancy was about to ask Susan if she wanted to join them when she remembered the run-in between Rob and Susan's new boyfriend earlier that afternoon.

As if Susan had read her thoughts, she said, "Um, Nancy, about that fight this afternoon . . . I'm sorry if Greg was rude. He's not such a bad guy, really, but he's never really liked Rob very much."

That was the understatement of the year, Nancy thought to herself. The question was, did Greg hate Rob enough to set him up for the jewel theft? "At least they didn't actually throw any punches," Nancy said. "Listen, I have to run—"

"Okay. You have your key. Have fun."

On the way to the restaurant, Nancy told the others about what had happened at the shed. "Anyway," she concluded, "one of the officers is going to come see me sometime tomorrow. Maybe I'll finally be able to convince them that Rob is being framed."

"I sure hope so," Rob said.

"Hey," Ned said. "You never told us what the police asked you at the library."

Rob shrugged. "The same old stuff. They kept telling me they think I stole the jewels, and I kept telling them I didn't."

La Fleur-de-Lis was just a block from the edge of campus. Jerry gave his name to the headwaiter, who said in an accented voice, "Would you mind waiting a few moments, Monsieur McEntee? Your table is almost ready." He showed them to a curved bench in a little alcove. A low wall topped by potted plants separated it from the dining room, which was decorated to look like a small French inn.

Nancy sat down on the bench. On the other side of the low wall, just behind her head, two men were speaking, and she was distracted by their conversation. One of the voices sounded familiar, but Nancy couldn't quite place it.

"We'd like to make a major move into sporting goods," the familiar voice was saying. "It's a good fit with our other activities."

"I don't know," the other man said. "I know my customers. One of the reasons they come to my store is that I know them and their kids. They're willing to pay a premium for personal attention, and they'll go elsewhere if they don't get it. I just can't become part of a chain." The man sounded unhappy and defensive.

"Look," the first man said, "you know what happens to people who stand in the way of progress. They get flattened. Of course, I might consider calling the deal off, *if* someone comes through with something."

"Hey, Nancy." She blinked as Jerry tapped her on the arm. "Are you still with us? You can forget about those stolen jewels for one evening, can't you?"

"And one morning," Ned added. "Don't forget we've got a skating date first thing tomorrow."

"Oh, I remember," Nancy assured him.

"You'll have a lot of fun," Bess said with a grin. "You'll be freezing your nose and toes down at the lake, while we're suffering through a warm, delicious breakfast."

Nancy groaned dramatically, then became silent as she realized that the conversation behind her had taken a very interesting turn. The men were now talking about the jewel theft!

"A terrible thing," the one with the familiar voice was saying. "I'm happy, of course, that I didn't lose anything, but it's a blow to the museum's reputation. If the jewels aren't recovered immediately, the museum won't attract other traveling exhibitions."

Just as Nancy realized whose voice she was listening to, the headwaiter reappeared. "Monsieur McEntee?" he said. "Your table is ready. If you would follow me?"

As she stood up, Nancy glanced over the row of potted plants. Sure enough, she found herself looking straight at William Whorf—and he was returning her gaze. Apparently he recognized her because he gave her a nod. Nancy barely had the presence of mind to smile. William Whorf, she thought. The diamond ring and stickpin he had been wearing at the museum opening—the museum director saying that Whorf was an avid collector of famous jewels—a new theory hit Nancy with the force of a Mack truck.

What if *Whorf* had stolen the empress's jewels to add to his private collection?

Chapter

Ten

NANCY'S HEAD WAS REELING as the headwaiter led their group to a table near the front of the restaurant. As she passed the table where Whorf and his companion were sitting, Nancy quickly studied the other man. He was no one she had ever met—she was sure of that—but somehow he, too, seemed familiar.

She racked her brain, but whatever the connection was, it kept slipping away from her. Whoever he was, it sounded as if Whorf was trying to pressure him into some kind of deal.

Nancy shook her head, pushing their conversation out of her mind and turning her attention to the long list of intriguing dishes on the menu. But she was so distracted that she barely tasted her sole amandine or heard the conversation at the table. It was more important than ever that she talk to Whorf. But since she couldn't do anything about it now, she decided to relax and enjoy the rest of her dinner.

"I think I've died and gone to heaven," Bess exclaimed, as she polished off the last bit of her filet mignon with béarnaise sauce.

When they had finished their entrees, the waiter brought them the dessert menu. "Oooh, they have profiteroles," said Bess. "I had them once and nearly died! Imagine, a plateful of tiny pastries like cream puffs but filled with ice cream and covered with hot chocolate sauce."

"Imagine an extra five zillion calories," George said. "I think I'll just have the fruit cup."

"Hey," Jerry said, "how often do you come to Winter Carnival? I say we have profiteroles all around!"

George shook her head. "Not for me, thanks."

"Nor me," Nancy said. "I'll just share Bess's." She laughed at her friend's stricken look.

A light snow was starting to fall when they left the restaurant. The flakes glistened as they drifted past the street lamps. "This is a magical night," Nancy said. "If it weren't so late, I'd love to take a long walk through the snow."

Ned gave her a mysterious look. "I have a

better idea," he said, taking her arm. "A little surprise for everybody."

He led them back to Emerson Hall, an administration building that was the original home of the college. As they approached the building, Nancy heard the high-pitched sound of tiny bells and guessed Ned's surprise.

There in front of the hall was a horse-drawn sleigh of red and green with gold trim. The driver, who was wearing a long black cloak and a top hat, got down from his seat to help them in. There were two wide seats, both facing forward.

Jerry turned to Ned. "Why don't we all scrunch into the front seat and let you and Nancy have the rear one? Is that okay?"

"Sure," Ned agreed. "But will you have enough room?"

"If we don't, that's part of the fun," Jerry replied. He grinned at Bess, who blushed.

Nancy climbed up into the rear seat and sat down close to Ned. "What a wonderful idea this was," she murmured, nestling her head against his shoulder. She straightened up to let the driver cover their legs and feet with a plaid blanket of thick, warm wool, then settled back again.

"Does anybody know what the temperature is?" Bess asked.

Jerry wet his finger and held it up. "Below freezing," he said.

"I already knew that," Bess protested. "Say, your hands must be cold. Don't you have gloves?"

"Sure, lots of them," he replied. "And they're all back at the frat house."

The driver climbed into his seat and announced, "Here we go." He shook the reins, and the horse tossed its head and began to pull. As the sleigh moved off into the night, the bells sewn to its harness rang out merrily.

Ned leaned forward and said to the others, "I asked the driver to take us once around College Woods. It should be very pretty just now."

"The whole campus is beautiful," George said. "Too bad we're here for only two more days."

"You can always come back," Rob said. Then he, too, sat back to enjoy the ride. Glimpsing the warm look he gave George, Nancy decided that Bess and Jerry weren't the only ones who were getting along well.

As they turned onto one of the fire lanes that led through College Woods, Bess said, "It's so picture-perfect. I know—why don't we sing something? Any ideas?"

Jerry chuckled. "I hate to mention it," he said, "but this *is* 'a one-horse open sleigh.' Ho, ho, ho. 'Jingle Bells' and all that."

"You've got to be kidding," Rob said.

"No way am I singing 'Jingle Bells,'" George said. "There are limits."

Bess turned to her cousin. "Aw, come on." She began to launch into song, and Jerry joined in. Nancy noticed that despite George's grumbling, she and Rob soon were singing, too.

Nancy tilted her head up and whispered into Ned's ear, "What do you say we skip the song?"

"Good idea," he whispered back, tightening his arm around her. Then his lips met hers, and she forgot about everything except how wonderful it felt to be with Ned.

Too soon, the sleigh was pulling up in front of Emerson Hall again. Two couples were waiting on the steps for the sleigh. As Nancy climbed down, she saw that one of the couples was Susan and Greg. She glanced nervously over at Rob. Would he and Greg get into another argument? But Rob was in the middle of an intense conversation with George. Either he didn't notice Greg and Susan or he was doing a good job of pretending not to see them.

As Susan passed Nancy on her way to the sleigh, she smiled and asked, "How did you like the ride?"

"It was great," Nancy replied. "Cold but great."

"Here, take this back, so you won't freeze,"

Greg said, wrapping his orange and purple muffler around Susan's neck. She settled her chin into the wool muffler, then looked at Nancy again. "You're not still planning to go skating early in the morning, are you?" she asked.

"Sure, it'll be fun," Nancy said.

Before Susan could respond, the sleigh driver shook the reins. The horse gave a snort and a faint whinny and started down the lane.

After walking back to the dorm, Nancy, Bess, and George said good night to the guys and then turned in for the night. As Nancy drifted off to sleep, the image of Whorf and his companion kept swirling in her mind, and she resolved once again to try to talk to him the next day.

The *brrrring!* of Nancy's travel alarm brought her up out of a deep sleep. She pushed back the covers, sat up, and reached for her penlight on the floor next to the bed. Moving as silently as possible so as not to wake the others, she found her toilet kit and towel and started to tiptoe toward the door. Bess and George were sound asleep in their sleeping bags, but Susan was already up and gone. She hadn't been kidding when she told Nancy she was an early riser. It was only six o'clock!

By the time she was dressed and ready, Ned was downstairs waiting. He gave her a good-morning kiss, then handed her a cardboard container of cocoa. "I stopped by the all-night diner on the way over," he explained.

Nancy lifted the lid and took a sip of cocoa. "This is perfect," she said.

"It's going to be a beautiful day," Ned said, zipping up his parka. "Clear and crisp. Let's not waste a moment of it."

"You're right," Nancy replied, taking Ned's arm. "It *is* a beautiful day."

On the walk down to the lake, the only sound was the crunch of their boots on the snow. Overhead the sky was still dark blue, but to the east it was brightening quickly.

When they reached the lake's edge Nancy brushed a dusting of fresh snow off the log bench and sat down to put on her skates. Soon she and Ned were moving over the frosty ice.

"It's nice having the lake to ourselves, isn't it?" Ned remarked, skating up beside her and coming to a stop.

"It sure is," Nancy replied. With an impish grin, she tapped him on the arm and added, "Let's play tag. You're It."

She took off down the ice, then risked a quick glance over her shoulder. Ned, taken by surprise, was just starting to move. She had a huge head start. Laughing, she picked up her pace. Ned was calling to her, but the wind tore his words away.

On her right, the boat house zipped by. Suddenly she began to feel unsteady, as if the surface of the ice was different.

Nancy gasped as she realized what had happened. The barriers—the Thin Ice sign—where were they? She peered frantically ahead and to either side, but they were nowhere in sight.

A loud crack, like that of a pistol shot, cut the crisp air. The frozen surface of the lake was shifting under her skates!

Chapter

Eleven

N ANCY!" NED SHOUTED from behind her. "Nancy, stop!"

Nancy swerved sharply to the left and leaned hard into the turn, feeling the edges of her skate blades bite into the ice. A fine spray of ice particles showered across the surface, then, miraculously, she was standing still.

Still but not yet safe. She held her breath and kept absolutely motionless. The ice under her was rocking unsteadily. From all around came loud popping sounds like those from little kids firing off cap pistols. A crack appeared less than a yard from her skates and started to widen.

"This way," Ned called. He was standing a dozen feet away, an agonized, worried look on his face. "Quick!"

Nancy was afraid to move, for fear that the ice would break, but she knew she couldn't just stand there. She took a deep breath and looked around her. To her right was a patch of ice that looked solid—for the moment, at least.

Knowing it might mean disaster, she pushed off and skated, trying to avoid the obvious weak spots. She fought a desire to hurry. Any sudden movements could cause the ice to crack open. She was less than a yard from Ned when the blade on her left skate broke through.

Panic surged through her as she lunged forward and caught Ned's outstretched hands. He pulled her away from the area of greatest danger and then hugged her tightly.

"You could have died, Nan!" he exclaimed. "Didn't you hear me calling you?"

"Yes," Nancy told him. "But I couldn't hear what you were saying. Anyway, by then it was almost too late." She shivered, looking back at the treacherous area of ice now riddled with huge cracks. Frowning, she said angrily, "What I'd like to know is, what happened to the sign and the sawhorses?"

A few minutes later she and Ned found the sawhorses and the Thin Ice sign lying in the snow near the boat house dock. They set them up again, a safe distance from the dangerous area.

"What kind of idiot removed those barriers?" Ned said. "We could have had a serious accident."

"That was no accident," Nancy said.

"You don't think someone deliberately took them away, someone who knew that we were coming down to skate this morning?" Ned was silent for a moment, then burst out, "Come on, Nancy! Who'd do a thing like that?"

"Who?" she said, pausing at the edge of the ice. "I don't have a name yet, but I know what the person's like. It's somebody who wanted to scare me and never stopped to think that this method might be fatal. Or else it's someone who simply doesn't care."

As she was pulling on her snowboots a bit later, she added, "Someone who doesn't know or doesn't care what their actions do to others is very dangerous. He or she has to be stopped."

"But who do you think it is?" Ned said, sitting down close to her.

Nancy raised both hands and tucked her reddish blond hair behind her ears in a distracted motion. "It has to be someone who knew we were planning to come skating early this morning."

Ned wrinkled his forehead and drew his eyebrows together. "Hmmm— Wait, I've got it! It must be Greg! Remember? Last night, after our sleigh ride, Susan asked you if you were still planning to go skating first thing. And Greg was right there, listening!"

"So were their two friends," Nancy pointed out. "Not to mention Susan herself, and George, Bess, Jerry, and Rob. That doesn't narrow down the possibilities a whole lot." She tapped her mittened hand against her knee. "Try to remember. When else did we talk about skating?"

Ned thought for a moment. "Last night at the restaurant, didn't Bess make some crack about how you'd be freezing out here at the crack of dawn this morning?"

"You're right." Nancy leaned forward. "It was while we were waiting for our table. And do you know who was right in back of us, close enough to hear everything? William Whorf!"

Ned looked blank.

"Whorf," Nancy repeated. "The guy who made the speech at the museum. The trustee. The famous jewelry collector! He knows I'm investigating the theft. *And* he's a complete nut about collecting famous jewelry. What if *he* was responsible for the robbery, and now he wants to keep us from investigating?"

"That makes sense," Ned said, slowly nodding. "But how are we ever going to prove it?"

"I don't know," Nancy admitted. She stood up and slung her skates over her shoulder. "I'm going to try to talk to him, but I don't know if it will get me anywhere. Come on. Let's go back and talk it over with the others. Maybe one of them will have a good idea."

They found George and Bess in the student cafeteria, having breakfast. "All by yourselves?" Ned asked in surprise.

"Rob needs some study time, and Jerry has to run some errands," Bess replied. "How was your skating date?"

"More exciting than we would have liked," Nancy replied as she and Ned sat down. She quickly told them about her near accident. Then she told them about her suspicions of Whorf.

"But, Nancy," George protested, "the theft happened during or right after the fire in the boat house."

"That's right," Nancy replied. "That was when the museum guards were distracted and the alarm system was turned off."

"Then I don't see how Whorf can be the thief," George said. "He was with the other speakers at the dedication of the new rowing tank."

Nancy thought back to the ceremony the previous morning. "You're absolutely right," she said. "As a matter of fact, the coach had just finished

103

thanking him when we noticed the smoke coming in from the boat house. So much for my bright idea."

"Hold on," Bess said. "What if he hired somebody to steal the jewels for him? Of course he'd arrange to be somewhere else, in plain sight, when it happened."

"You're right," Nancy told her. "An important, well-known man like Whorf would probably find someone else to do his dirty work. I can't see him sneaking down to the lake to remove those sawhorses, but I can imagine him telling somebody else to do it."

Maybe that was where Greg fit in, she added to herself. She decided not to say anything to the others, though—not until she had more proof.

"I'll tell you what," Ned said, glancing at his watch. "You remember Frazier, the redheaded guy who was in the museum? He's a reporter at the Emerson radio station. I'm going to hunt him up. I bet the station has background files on the trustees of the college. Maybe I can find something in Whorf's file."

"Good idea," Nancy replied. "If you don't find us here, we'll be down working on our snow sculptures." She grinned at him. "I wouldn't want the judges to be disappointed in my work."

Ned reached over to ruffle her hair, then stood up and headed for the cafeteria door. "Anybody for more coffee or tea?" she started to ask, as a frantic voice interrupted.

"Are you Nancy Drew?"

Nancy turned to see a heavyset guy with a worried look on his round face. "Yes. Is something wrong?"

"Rob Harper asked me to find you right away. It's the police," the guy said. "They just came into my room—I mean Rob's room. We're roommates. Anyway, they have a search warrant, and I think they're planning to arrest Rob!"

Bess's eyes widened, and George nearly choked on the sip of coffee she was taking. "I can't believe it," George said. "Can't they leave the poor guy alone?"

"Don't worry," Nancy said, patting George's shoulder. Turning back to Rob's roommate, she said, "We'd better go back with you and find out exactly what's going on."

When they got to Rob's room, Sergeant Balsam was there, taking books off the shelves and peering behind them. Another police officer was going through Rob's dresser drawers, while a third was examining the closet. Rob was sitting dejectedly on a bed, his head in his hands. When he saw Nancy, he jumped to his feet. "Boy, am I glad to see you!"

Nancy gave him an encouraging smile as she, Bess, and George stepped into the room. "We came to offer moral support." She turned to Sergeant Balsam and asked, "Is there some new evidence? Is that why you're searching Rob's room?"

The sergeant ignored her.

"What are you looking for, anyway?" Rob asked. "There's nothing here for you to find."

Balsam didn't answer. He finished with the bookshelves and sat down to look through Rob's desk drawers.

"Why are you picking on me?" Rob asked. "How am I supposed to bring my grades up with all this going on? It's not fair!"

Nancy sympathized with Rob, but she could tell he was only making the situation worse. As the sergeant left the desk and began to look under the mattress of Rob's bed, one of the other policemen picked up Rob's tan parka.

A frown came over the officer's face as he reached into one of the pockets. He pulled something out, but Nancy couldn't see what it was.

"Sergeant?" the officer said quietly.

"You got something?" Balsam said.

The officer stretched out his right hand and opened it. Nancy gasped. In his palm, a ruby and diamond earring glittered.

"That's one of the empress's earrings from the museum!" Bess exclaimed.

Chapter

Twelve

SERGEANT BALSAM and Nancy stepped over at the same time to get a closer look at the earring.

"Where did you find it?" Balsam demanded.

"It was inside the left-hand pocket of this parka," the officer replied.

The sergeant turned to Rob. "Is this your parka?"

Rob looked stunned. "Why, yes, sure. But I never—"

Balsam pulled a small card out of his shirt pocket and began to read. " 'You have the right to remain silent. You—' "

"Sergeant," Nancy cut in urgently. "Before you go any further, may I look at that earring?"

Balsam frowned at her a moment, then said, "Okay, but no funny business."

The police officer held up the earring. Nancy peered at it, then bent to see the back. "Doesn't that stud fastener look awfully modern to you, Sergeant?" she asked.

"That's not something I know a lot about," the sergeant replied in an even tone.

Nancy leaned in so that her face almost touched the police officer's hand, and then straightened up. "Sergeant," she said, "I'm no expert, either. But I'm ready to bet you that the Empress of Austria didn't wear ruby earrings stamped 'Made in Hong Kong'!"

"What! Here, let me see that!" Balsam sputtered. He grabbed the earring from the officer and carried it over to the window, where the light was better. When he turned back, his face was red with anger and embarrassment.

"All right, so this is a fake," he admitted grudgingly. "But don't forget that the thief replaced the stolen jewelry with fakes that looked a lot like this, to delay discovery of the theft. This earring may not be part of the loot, but it's evidence just the same."

"I never saw it before!" Rob protested.

Nancy put her hand on his arm. "It wouldn't matter even if you had," she told him. "There's no law against having a piece of costume jewelry in your pocket. Am I right, Sergeant Balsam?"

He gave her a look in which she saw grudging respect mixed with his irritation. "That's right. But I'm going to hold on to this earring all the same. I'll give you a receipt," he told Rob.

"It's not mine," Rob insisted. "I don't want a receipt."

Balsam paid no attention. He scribbled out the receipt and handed it to Rob, who stared at it as if it were poison.

Balsam turned to his officers. "Are you done in here?" he asked. When they nodded, he said, "Okay, let's move out."

Nancy followed the police to the door. "Sergeant, have you decided to check out that gas can?" she asked. "I really think—"

He held up his hand. "I know, I know. It's an important clue. Well, Ms. Drew, it's not really any of your business, but we went by that shed this morning and collected the gas can. It's empty, by the way, and it has no fingerprints whatsoever on it."

Nancy stared. "But, Sergeant, don't you see why there aren't any prints? Because somebody carefully wiped them off!"

"I thought of that," Balsam said patiently. "Also it's wintertime, and around here people wear gloves when they're outside. Now, if you'll excuse me, I have a lot to do."

He turned and started to leave, but Nancy said, "Wait a minute. Don't you want the museum label I found yesterday?"

Sergeant Balsam paused long enough to take the white label she held out. He stuffed it in his pocket without looking at it, then followed his two officers down the stairs.

When Nancy reentered Rob's room, he said, "If it hadn't been for you, he would have arrested me."

"He doesn't really have anything you could call evidence, just some peculiar circumstances." She put a hand on his arm. "Rob, there's something I need to know. Where did you get that earring?"

"Nancy, I never saw that earring before in my life," he said earnestly.

She nodded. "That's what I thought. After all, if you'd known the earring was in your pocket, you would have thrown it away rather than get caught with it. The question is, when and how did it find its way into your pocket?"

"The last time I wore the parka was to the restaurant last night. And all day yesterday after my crew jacket disappeared."

"Where did you leave it at the restaurant?" asked Bess.

"On the coatrack near the door." Rob shook his head. "This is hopeless. Anybody could have planted that earring in my pocket."

"Anybody who was at the restaurant," George said.

Nancy thought immediately of Whorf. He had seen them come in, and he had to have passed the coatrack when he left while they were still having dinner and their coats were still hanging there. But Nancy couldn't be sure Whorf knew Rob, even by sight.

Bess wrinkled her brow. "Do you really think the earring could have been in your pocket all evening without your knowing it?" she asked.

"What are you trying to say?" Rob retorted. "That I knew about it? That I had something to do with the theft?"

"No, of course not," Bess said. She looked taken aback by the force of his reply. "But if we're trying to figure out when and where it was put there, it'd help to know when it *wasn't* there. Am I right?" she added, turning to Nancy.

"Sounds good to me," Nancy said. "Rob, can you remember how often you reached into that pocket?"

"Sure," he said promptly. "Practically never. Since I'm usually wearing gloves, I hardly ever use the pockets to keep my hands warm. For all I know, the earring could have been there for weeks."

"Hmmm," Nancy said. "I was hoping that something about this case would turn out to be simple. Still, the business with the earring does tell us one thing. The thief is still around, and the stolen jewels probably are, too."

"Why do you say that?" George asked.

"Why would anyone try to frighten me off if he'd already gotten rid of the jewels? Also, the thief left so many false clues incriminating Rob that the police have spent all their time questioning him."

"Okay," Bess said, "but where does that take us?"

"How about this?" Nancy replied. She began pacing back and forth as she spoke. "The thief is still on campus. Whoever it is can't leave right away without creating suspicion—or maybe the thief put the jewels in a safe hiding place and has to wait to retrieve them. Framing Rob is meant to keep the police busy and distract them from looking too hard elsewhere on campus. Then, when we started investigating, the thief felt very threatened." She paused and faced the others, who were looking at her expectantly. "I think we can expect more tries at planting evidence against Rob and at scaring us off."

"Creepy!" said George. "And I thought we were coming here for a fun weekend!"

"We can still have fun," Nancy said. "We just have to be careful."

"Oh, no," Bess said. "Ned and Jerry are expecting to meet us down at the lake. I bet they're wondering what's happened to us."

Just then, there was a knock on the door, which opened slightly. "Hey, Rob," Jerry said. "Have you seen—" His gaze landed on the girls. "There you are. We got cold waiting by the lake, so we decided to come look for you."

When Ned and Jerry heard about the search warrant and the earring, Ned said, "We'd better solve this case fast if we want to keep Rob out of jail."

Rob cleared his throat and said, "Look, I really appreciate what you're doing, all of you. But I don't want you to ruin your weekend just because of this mess I'm in."

"How about this," Ned said, "the rest of the morning, we try to get more evidence to clear Rob. Then, after lunch, we tear ourselves away from the case and do something carnival-y—and that includes you, Detective Drew," Ned added sternly.

"How about hitting the slopes?" Jerry suggested. "It's a good day for it."

Seeing their eager expressions, Nancy let out a resigned laugh. "Sounds good to me," she said.

* * *

Three hours later Nancy was in Susan's dorm room, fastening the shoulder strap of her new turquoise ski overalls. She quickly checked her reflection in the mirror. The color of her outfit made her eyes seem even more blue.

It had taken longer than she expected to try to get in touch with Whorf. She got an answering service, and they refused to put her call through or give her his home phone number. She hadn't made any progress at all, and now she was late to meet the rest of the gang downstairs.

She was just reaching for her skis when Susan came in.

"Hi," Susan said, brightly. "Great overalls. Going skiing?"

"Yes," Nancy replied, smiling. "Do you want to join us?"

"I wish I could, but I'm working at the museum all afternoon," Susan replied.

"Too bad. And you were up so early this morning, too. Don't you ever get a chance to goof off and relax?"

Susan seemed surprised by the question. She looked down, then mumbled, "Yeah—I mean, sure."

Nancy gave her a curious look, then remembered that everyone was still waiting for her. "Well, I'll see you later." Gathering up her equipment, she left the room.

All six of them managed to squeeze themselves and their ski equipment into Jerry's battered sedan for the half-hour drive to the ski area. At the base lodge, they put on their boots, then stacked their skis on the rack outside while they went into the lodge to buy lift tickets.

In line, Nancy glanced through the big windows of the lodge snack bar, then did a double-take. She was staring right into the eyes of William Whorf. Whorf quickly lowered his glance, but Nancy knew he had recognized her before looking away.

They were nearly to the ticket booth when Ned said, "Look, Rob, there's one of your favorite people. Try to keep cool, okay?"

Greg, Susan's boyfriend, was just pushing off toward the chair lift.

"The earring!" Rob exclaimed. "He must have slipped it in my pocket the other night at the student center. That's why he wanted to pick a fight with me!"

He made a move as if to leave the line and go after Greg, but Ned grabbed his arm. "Not now," he said. "We're supposed to be having fun, remember?"

Rob grumbled but remained with the group as they got their passes and headed for the slopes. As the chair lift carried Nancy and Ned up the hill, she thought about Rob's accusation. She was becoming more and more positive that Greg was the thief they were looking for. He was probably the one Whorf had gotten to do his dirty work. Greg certainly had a grudge. Something was nagging at her, though—some detail she couldn't quite remember. But what?

At the top of the slope, she wiggled her shoulders to loosen up, did a couple of knee bends, and glanced over at Ned. "Ready?" she asked.

He nodded, and she pushed off. The snow was great, several inches of powder over a firm base, and she adjusted her line to pick up speed. Noticing a small mogul just in front of her, Nancy crouched lower, then sprang up as she swooped up it. Grinning, she felt herself become airborne.

In a flash, Nancy realized that something was terribly wrong. Her right ski! It had come loose! In another instant she was going to hit the ground with one ski on and the other dangling at the end of the safety strap, and there wasn't a thing she could do about it!

Chapter

Thirteen

Nᴀɴᴄʏ ɢʀɪᴛᴛᴇᴅ ʜᴇʀ ᴛᴇᴇᴛʜ and gripped her ski poles tightly, preparing herself for what was sure to be a disastrous crash.

Just in time, she positioned her right foot in back of the heel binding of her left ski and bent both knees to cushion the impact.

She crashed into the slope, managing to stay upright for half a second before her right ski smashed to the ground and threw her off balance. The breath was knocked out of her as she hit the ground, but she didn't think she had injured herself.

Looking ahead, she saw that she was sliding

dangerously close to the woods that edged the slope. She quickly held out her poles so that they dragged in the snow. After a flurried moment she was sitting up at the edge of the woods, rubbing a spot on her hip.

Ned, white-faced, schussed up and stopped in a shower of snow. "Nancy, are you all right?" he cried. "What happened?"

"Another 'accident,'" she said grimly. She reached down for the ski that had fallen off and began to examine the binding. "I'm okay, but only because of incredible good luck. Someone must have tampered with this binding. Look, it releases at the slightest pressure!"

Ned took the ski from her and wiggled the heel lock from side to side. "It's loose, all right," he confirmed. "Could it just have been badly adjusted?"

"I had the bindings checked at the beginning of the season," Nancy replied. "And I know they were okay a couple of weeks ago. Here, let me see if I can fix it well enough to get down the hill."

As she was working on the binding, Bess, George, Jerry, and Rob appeared. Ned told them what had happened.

"Greg!" Rob exclaimed, his face becoming red with anger. "Remember? When we saw him, he was coming from the direction of the ski rack. He must have just finished sabotaging Nancy's skis!"

"Maybe," Nancy said slowly. "But I have another candidate—William Whorf. He was at the base lodge, too, and he saw me leave my skis on the rack, when we went to buy tickets.

"There," she added, laying the ski on the ground and fitting her boot into it. She stamped the ski on the snow a few times, and it held. "That should stay on for one run. I hope there's someone at the pro shop who can do a proper adjustment. I'm not about to let some saboteur spoil our ski date!"

A few hours later, as they were walking back to the parking lot, Ned said, "Do you really suspect Whorf? I talked to Frazier about him this morning, but I don't know if I learned anything that will help. About the only new thing I found out is that his businesses have been expanding a lot in the past few years."

Nancy turned that over in her mind. That fit with what she'd overheard the past night. Whorf must have been trying to convince the other guy to join one of his growing business chains. Still, it didn't help her case any.

"That doesn't give us much to go on," she admitted, "but I just know he's involved. There's got to be some evidence I'm overlooking—something that ties him to the crimes. But what?"

Taking off her mittens, she jammed them into the pockets of her coat in frustration. As she did so, her fingers brushed the zippered pocket and she remembered the scrap of yarn from the night before. She pulled it out and studied it.

"Ned," she said excitedly, turning toward him. "What do you see here?"

He bent down to look. "It looks like a piece of orange wool," he said.

"All orange?"

"Well, it's hard to tell, but there might be a hint of bluish purple, too, up at that end."

"In other words, orange and purple—the Emerson College colors. Last night Greg Forsyte was wearing a wool scarf in those colors. I bet he was the one who tried to lock me in the shed!"

"A lot of Emerson students have scarves like that," Ned warned. "I don't think it proves much."

"Maybe not," Nancy replied.

When they caught up to the others, who were waiting by the car, George announced, "We've decided to do some work on our snow sculptures after we drop off our ski stuff." She glanced at Rob. "I know mine's not nearly finished."

"Good idea," Nancy said. While she was molding snow, she might be able to turn over the facts and evidence in her mind. She still had the feeling there was something important that she was overlooking.

An hour later Nancy had all but completed her snowman, but she still hadn't come up with anything new. Maybe you're trying too hard, she told herself. Sometimes clues fell into place when she least expected them to. She might as well try to relax and enjoy herself.

The dance that night was the biggest event of Winter Carnival. The three girls dressed up for the occasion. Nancy and George both wore sweater dresses, Nancy's in blue green, and George's in a soft brown, while Bess wore a black wool minidress with a scooped neck. They arrived at Emerson's gym a little after nine o'clock.

The gym had been transformed for the dance. The entrance of the huge room was decorated to look like an arctic scene. There were igloos, reindeer, seals, and even a glittering glacier.

Bess looked around and shivered. "I feel colder here than I did outside!" she joked.

"Let's check out the rest of the place," Jerry suggested.

He took Bess's hand and led her through the huge room, with the rest of the group following behind. The decor changed dramatically from one end to the other. The bandstand, in the center, could have come from a small town before the turn of the century. The refreshment tables, at the far end, were set up in Polynesian grass huts among tall tropical palms.

They found a table for six. Then Ned took Nancy's hand and pulled her onto the dance floor. When they returned, Jerry and Bess were alone at the table, chatting and laughing.

"Where's George?" Nancy asked.

Jerry blinked. "George? Oh—she and Rob decided to dance," he said, waving vaguely toward the bandstand. "I guess they aren't back yet."

"Oh, listen," Bess said. "I love this tune. Why don't we dance, too?"

Jerry took her hand, and they vanished into the crowd of dancers. Ned met Nancy's gaze and started to laugh. "I'm not much good as a matchmaker, am I?" he said.

"You did a great job—except that you got things backward," Nancy replied with a laugh. "And, anyway, they seem to have managed to work things out themselves. As far as I can tell, everyone seems happy."

Ned interlaced his fingers with hers and pulled her closer. "Especially me," he said.

"Nancy, guess what?" George interrupted, as she and Rob came over. "Rob has promised to teach me sculling. Isn't that great? I've always loved boats."

"It'll have to wait until spring, of course, when the ice melts," Rob said. A smile lit up his face. "I'm glad Coach didn't decide to take away my key when he suspended me from crew. At least I can still go out rowing on my own."

Nancy stared at him. In her mind she flashed back to the fire, remembering how the fire fighters had pried open the doors to the boat house.

"It was locked!" she exclaimed. Her friends looked at her as if she were crazy. "The boat house," she quickly added. "It was locked. Whoever set the fire must have had a key!"

"Don't tell the police that," Rob said quickly. "They'd arrest me for sure!"

"You're not the only one with a key, are you?" Nancy demanded.

"No, of course not. There must be a half a dozen of us who have them, so we can go sculling at times when the boat house is locked."

Nancy took a deep breath. "How about Greg Forsyte?" she asked. "Does he have one?"

Rob frowned. "Greg? I'm not sure. He's not on the varsity crew, but one or two of the JV guys . . ." His voice died away.

"Well?" Nancy prompted.

"I remember," Rob said, brightening. "Once

last fall I went down to the boat house very early. It was already unlocked, and Greg was carrying out a shell. He must have had a key. Hey, there he is, right over there."

Nancy looked up sharply and saw Greg walking toward the refreshment area with the stride of someone who had a purpose. Some instinct made Nancy stand up, mutter, "I'll be right back," and take off after him.

A blond guy carrying five paper cups of soda stepped in front of her, and she lost sight of Greg. Finally she managed to brush by him and plunge ahead.

Where was he? There! He was heading back toward the dance floor. She hurried after him, and when he paused, she stepped behind the crowd of kids to watch.

Greg was less than a dozen feet away—and he was talking to William Whorf! What was Whorf doing at a student dance? Greg and Whorf seemed to be very intent on their conversation. Whorf pulled a white envelope from his pocket and handed it to Greg. Greg glanced around, shoved the envelope into the inside pocket of his jacket, and shook Whorf's hand.

From her hiding place, Nancy stared in amazement. She couldn't be positive, but she was fairly sure she had just witnessed the payoff for the jewelry theft!

Chapter

Fourteen

NANCY CONTINUED TO WATCH closely. After another brief exchange with Whorf, Greg strode off. Whorf watched him for a moment, a smug smile on his face, then strolled away. Nancy followed, careful to keep a screen of people between them to conceal her if he should look back.

After five minutes of following him around the gym, Nancy began to wonder if she was wasting her time. Whorf didn't seem to be going anywhere. He nodded to a few people, but he didn't stop to talk to any of them. He seemed more interested in the decorations than anything else.

"Hey, Nancy," a voice called out. She caught

her breath, hoping Whorf hadn't heard and looked around. Bess was hurrying toward her with a look of concern on her face. "We were worried about you," Bess continued, taking Nancy's arm. "Nobody knew where you'd gone."

"I'm following someone," Nancy said in an undertone. "Tell everybody I'll be back as soon as I can."

"Oh—sure. Sorry." Bess glanced around like a bad actress in a spy movie before backing away.

Nancy turned around again and spotted Whorf at a table on the sidelines, sitting on the edge of a chair and talking with an older couple. The man looked familiar. He was deeply tanned, and the lines around his eyes gave him the appearance of someone who was used to gazing across distances. Nancy suddenly recalled that she had seen him on the speakers' stand at the boat house the day before. He was the crew coach. But what—?

Nancy's eyes widened. Whorf was pulling an envelope from his pocket, exactly like the envelope he had given to Greg. He handed it to the coach, who glanced at the envelope and put it on the table. The two men stood up and shook hands, and then, after a word to the woman at the table, Whorf walked away.

Nancy took a few steps after him, then caught herself. What was more important at this point was learning what those envelopes contained. She had been so sure that Greg had stolen the jewels for Whorf, but now she was forced to wonder if her theory was correct. Was it possible that the crew coach was involved in the theft from the museum, too?

The coach, still on his feet, leaned over and said something to the woman, who smiled and stood up. The two of them walked toward the dance floor, leaving Whorf's envelope sitting on the table.

The opportunity was too good to pass up. Nancy walked quickly past the table and, without even breaking her stride, whisked up the envelope. She didn't stop until she had gone past another group of tables, a dozen paces away.

Casually, she scanned the area. Once she'd confirmed that no one was watching her, she studied the envelope. Her heart sank. It was unsealed. If it was an illicit message, wouldn't Whorf seal the envelope? Lifting the flap, she slipped out the paper.

Nancy felt her cheeks flush. It was an invitation to a party Whorf was giving in honor of the Emerson College rowing crews. So *that* was the "payoff" she had seen Whorf pass to Greg! That was probably why he had come in the first place, to hand out the invitations.

She quickly put the invitation back in its

envelope and dropped the envelope on the coach's table without being spotted. Then Nancy walked back to her own table. Ned was waiting for her.

She sat down next to him and told him about Whorf, Greg, and the party invitation. He listened sympathetically, then said, "But you could still be right about Greg being Whorf's accomplice, couldn't you? That envelope—"

Nancy sat bolt upright and grabbed Ned's arm. "No!" she exclaimed. "I just remembered— Greg *couldn't* be the thief. He's on the junior varsity crew. At the time of the theft, he and the rest of the JV's were getting ready to demonstrate the new rowing tank, in front of about two hundred people!"

Ned nodded. "You're right," he said. "I never thought of that."

"And I hadn't met Greg yet, so I didn't even notice him." Nancy pounded her fist on her thigh in frustration. "But if he couldn't have done it, and Whorf couldn't have, who did? Rob ducked out of the ceremony, so he *could* have been at the museum at the right time, but I refuse to think—"

"Hi," George said, approaching the table, "did you find out anything helpful?"

"That depends," Nancy replied. "I just managed to eliminate my main suspect, if you call that helpful."

Nancy saw the smile on Rob's face disappear. She was about to explain what had happened when the band launched into a slow, dreamy tune. Ned took her hand and said, "You need something to take your mind off this case, like trying to keep me from stepping on your feet. Let's dance."

Susan and Greg were also on the dance floor. As Nancy and Ned passed them, Nancy looked over at Susan. At that instant, Whorf walked by in the background, and Nancy did a double-take. Whorf and Susan hadn't even seemed to notice each other, but something about seeing them together jarred Nancy's memory. What was it? Had she ever seen them together? She ran over in her mind the occasions when she had seen Whorf. There were the ceremonies at the museum and the boat house, the French restaurant, the ski area, and now the dance. But Susan had never been with him.

Still, Nancy's thoughts kept circling back to Whorf and Susan. She could almost see them facing each other, talking in low voices, turning to glance at her . . .

That was it!

Nancy stopped so suddenly that Ned was

thrown off balance and had to jump back to avoid landing on her feet.

"What—?" he began.

"In the restaurant last night," Nancy said urgently. "The man having dinner with Whorf— did he remind you of anyone?"

"I didn't really notice," Ned said.

Nancy's blue eyes flashed. "He looked a lot like Susan, and I'd seen him before in a photograph on her dresser. I'm willing to bet that he's Susan's father. Come on, let's get back to the table. I hate to interrupt everyone's good time, but I'm going to need some help from you guys."

Ten minutes later Nancy used her key to let herself and George into Susan's room. Bess was downstairs, watching in case Susan came back early, while the three guys were still at the gym, keeping an eye on Susan, Greg, and Whorf.

Nancy switched on the light and threw the bolt on the door.

"What exactly are we looking for?" George asked in a whisper.

"We don't have to whisper," Nancy replied in a normal tone. "We have a right to be here." She took a deep breath and added, "First I want another look at the photo on the dresser."

"It's not there anymore." George pointed to the dresser top, which was clear except for a bottle of perfume and some toiletries. "That's weird. I definitely remember seeing it the day we arrived," she went on. "I wonder why she'd move it?"

"If my theory's right, it's because there's something in the photo Susan didn't want us to see—something that could give her a motive for the jewel theft!"

Nancy began to look through the drawers, feeling under the shirts and sweaters for anything that didn't belong. George went over to the bookcase and looked behind the books there.

In the middle dresser drawer, Nancy found a small jewelry box covered in imitation leather. She lifted the lid, then said, "George, come look."

George glanced over her shoulder and gasped. "A bracelet of rubies and diamonds. Bingo!"

"Red and clear glass," Nancy corrected. "But it looks awfully familiar. . . ." She turned over the bracelet and peered at the clasp. "'Made in Hong Kong,'" she read.

"Maybe it's part of a set with the earring that the police found in Rob's parka," George said.

"Susan could have planted it," Nancy said slowly. "Remember when she tripped and fell against him at the student center? I'll bet that was all an act to give her a chance to slip the earring in his pocket!"

A feeling of excitement, of being near the end of the chase, was building in Nancy.

A few minutes later, George called out, "I found it!"

Nancy set down the suitcase she had been about to open and hurried over to the desk. "That's the photo, all right," she said. "And that's the man who was at the restaurant with Whorf last night.

"Where did you find the picture?" Nancy asked.

"At the back of the file drawer, under these old term papers," George replied, riffling through the stack of papers. "Hey, wait, here's another photo."

She pulled it out, took one look, and stared at Nancy. "Susan's father and Whorf together."

"That proves there's a connection," Nancy said. "There's a newspaper clipping taped to the back. It says 'Financier William Whorf congratulates Frank Samuels on his new store, which will be the flagship of a planned chain of sporting goods stores.'"

"Big deal," George said. "That doesn't sound very incriminating to me."

"It's not hard proof, you're right. But listen to this." Nancy told George about the conversation she'd overheard between the two men at the restaurant. "It sounded like some kind of take-over," she finished, "and I didn't get the impression Mr. Samuels was happy about it."

George still looked confused. "I still don't see what that has to do with the theft and where Susan fits in."

"Remember the day we got here, how proud Susan was when you said what a great store Samuels for Sports was?" Nancy said. "She made a big deal out of the fact that her father had built it all up himself—"

"You're right!" George exclaimed. "She said he was the biggest *independent* sports store in the area."

"Well, maybe that's what's behind the theft. Listen to this. Whorf seems to have some kind of financial hold over Susan's father. What if Susan stole the jewels, planning to give them to Whorf so he'd leave her father alone?"

"That would be a strong motive, no question," George said. "And Rob's breakup with her gave her a motive to pin the theft on him."

"Right," Nancy said, slapping her fist into her palm. "Now, what else have we got? Means? Susan works at the museum. She knows how to set off a false alarm. *And* she would have known what the jewelry looked like far enough in advance to buy the fake stuff.

"As for opportunity, first, she could go in and out of the museum without attracting attention.

People were probably so used to seeing her there that they didn't really notice her before the theft, if they saw her at all. And afterward, when the exhibit area was empty, she probably made her getaway through the fire exit. Second, she could easily have taken Greg's boat house key, in order to set the fire." Nancy was ticking off each point on her fingers as she spoke. "And third, she knew about my skating date this morning. When I woke up, she was already gone. Where was she? Down at the lake, removing the barricades!"

"It all fits," George exclaimed. "Congratulations, Nancy. You've done it—you've cleared Rob and found the real thief!"

Nancy let out a long breath. Her mood of excitement left her as quickly as it had come. "Maybe," she said. "But we don't have a single shred of evidence. Unless we can recover the stolen jewels in Susan's possession."

"They're not in this room," George said. "I'm pretty sure of that. We've looked everywhere."

"I wouldn't expect them to be," Nancy replied. "Too unsafe. Besides—listen, George, she must have been on a split-second timetable. She had to set up the boat house fire, get back to the museum, set off the false alarm, steal the jewels the moment the fire engines arrived, and get off the premises before the theft was discovered. She couldn't have had time to go far with the jewels.

That means she must have hidden them somewhere near the museum until the commotion died down and it became safe to retrieve them."

Nancy snapped her fingers. "Right after the fire, we saw her working on her snow sculpture. Of course. It's the perfect place!"

George stared at her. "You think she hid the jewels in her sculpture?" she said. "Then all we have to do is go get them back!"

"No," Nancy said, shaking her head. "Then we'd have no evidence to link Susan to the theft. No, here's what I think we should do. . . ."

Nancy quickly explained her plan, and George's brown eyes gleamed with excitement.

"We've got her now," George said. "There's no way she'll be able to get out of this one!"

Chapter

Fifteen

NANCY SMOOTHED the cheek of her snowman with the back of her glove, then stepped away and looked around. Sunlight glinted off dozens of snow sculptures that edged the side of the lake. Nancy's was one of more than ten snowpeople. Other entries in the contest included an eight-foot smiling whale, a hungry-looking bear, and enough castles and forts to supply a medieval kingdom.

A big crowd had gathered to watch the judging of the contest, and a lot of contestants were still putting the finishing touches on their sculptures. On the far side of Bess's sculpture, Susan was standing next to a model of a sleigh that looked a lot like the one they had ridden in.

Nancy glanced casually at the sleigh, then at the other sculptures. It was vital that Susan not feel under suspicion, or even under surveillance.

A photographer from the campus newspaper asked Nancy to pose next to her entry, snapped a couple of exposures, and moved on to take a shot of George and her fort. A girl with a Press tag dangling from the zipper pull of her parka was videotaping the proceeding. Nancy smiled to herself. If they stayed until the end, they might find themselves with some really newsworthy material!

"Your attention, please," a bullhorn blared. "The judging of the Winter Carnival snow sculpture contest is now beginning. From this moment, contestants are not allowed to make changes to their entries."

Ned and his two fellow judges, armed with clipboards and ballpoint pens, began to make a circuit of the clearing. They stopped at each sculpture and made notes. They took their time, and Nancy found it hard to keep her patience. Her plan wouldn't go into action until after the preliminary round of judging.

As Ned and the other two judges slowly made their way through the sculptures, Nancy studied the crowd. Whorf was standing with Dean Jarvis and a couple of professors at the edge of the clearing. Nancy wondered what they would say if she told them that she suspected Whorf, a trustee and benefactor of the college, of being implicated in the theft from the museum.

Nancy was happy to see that Sergeant Balsam was also there. It had taken a lot of talking before she'd been able to convince him to show up.

Greg went over to stand with Susan, next to her sleigh. As Nancy watched, he took off his orange and purple scarf and tied it around Susan's neck. The gesture was an exact replay of what had happened in the sleigh the night before. Greg had put the scarf around Susan's neck, saying that he was *returning* it to her. *That* was what had been nagging at her. The scarf was Susan's, not Greg's, as she had suspected earlier. Nancy nodded. It had probably been Susan who shut her in the shed, too. One more piece of the puzzle fit into place.

Susan stiffened as Ned and the other two judges reached her entry. Ned examined the sleigh with particular care, squatting down to peer at the work.

Finally Ned stood up, nodded to the other judges, and led the way to Bess's castle. Just as they arrived, the tallest tower slipped sideways and collapsed.

"Oh, rats!" Bess exclaimed. The crowd laughed sympathetically, and a few people started to clap.

Nancy chuckled, but when she glanced back at Susan, she couldn't help staring. Susan looked terrified. Her mouth hung open, and her face was so pale that she looked ready to faint. Greg noticed and took her arm, but she shook him off.

Nancy frowned. Susan's reaction didn't make sense, but Nancy didn't have time to wonder why.

"Ahem!" Ned was now standing a couple of feet away from Nancy, in front of her snowman. "This contestant is"—he paused to check his clipboard—"Nancy Drew, of River Heights."

As if you didn't know! Nancy grinned at him, and he winked back. She stepped aside to let him and the other judges examine her snowman. They didn't seem very impressed. After making a few notes, they went on to George's fort. Nancy concentrated on Susan.

The bullhorn came to life again. "The judges have rated all the entries," Ned said. "But before we announce our decision, we have to make another, special examination of the sculptures."

The contestants seemed puzzled—all except Nancy, Bess, and George. But after all, the "special" examination had been Nancy's idea.

And she planned on keeping a careful eye on one person in particular, to see how she would react.

As she watched, it seemed to Nancy that Susan froze in place, as if she herself had become one of the snow sculptures.

"As all contestants know," Ned continued, "the contest rules state that only snow may be used in the sculptures. But rumors have reached us that some of the entries have been molded around wooden or wire frameworks. If that's so, we'll have to disqualify these. But first we have to know which ones they are."

"Get to the point, Nickerson," someone called from the crowd.

Ned held up a long stick. "Here's the point," he retorted. "We're going to go around and poke all the statues to make sure there's nothing but snow inside them."

"What? You'll wreck them," the same person called back.

"Rules are rules," Ned replied.

Nancy looked away from Susan for a moment and scanned the crowd behind her. Sergeant Balsam met her gaze and gave her a brief, almost imperceptible nod.

A lot of the spectators began following Ned around the field, blocking Nancy's view. She began to worry. She *had* to be in a position to see when the judges got to Susan's sleigh.

Nancy walked over and stood between Susan's and Bess's entries. When it was Susan's turn, Nancy watched intently as Ned and the other judges carefully inserted their sticks into the front, sides, and back of the sleigh, feeling for anything that wasn't snow. Most of the back seat of the sleigh fell down, then part of one side. When the judges were finished, it looked like little more than a pile of snow.

Ned caught Nancy's eye and shook his head slightly. She stared back at him in dismay.

She had been sure they would find the jewels there. But Ned had riddled the sleigh with holes. If anything had been hidden inside, he would have found it. Nancy pounded her gloved fist in her other hand. It had made so much sense—the timing, Susan's movements, everything! Where had she gone wrong?

Nancy felt a growing sense of alarm. Her plan had failed totally. Susan clearly had not hidden the jewels in her snow sculpture, and Nancy's case against her was slipping away. It was unbelievably frustrating! Nancy *knew* she was right, but still . . .

Taking a deep breath, she raced over the details in her mind. Susan hadn't seemed upset when Ned was poking her sculpture. But just before—

"Oh, no!" Nancy heard Bess shout. "Stop,

you're totally wrecking it!" A burst of laughter followed.

Nancy snapped to attention and fought her way to the front of the crowd. Someone had tripped and fallen right on top of Bess's castle and now was flailing around in the snow. Nancy immediately recognized the dark hair and the orange and purple scarf tied around the girl's neck.

As Susan stood up and started to turn, Nancy leapt forward and grabbed her wrist with both hands.

"Let go of me!" Susan screamed. "What are you doing?"

Nancy held on determinedly, gritting her teeth when the toe of Susan's boot hit her kneecap. "You can't get away now," she said through clenched teeth.

"Hey, let her alone!" Greg shouted. He started to shove Nancy away, but a moment later Ned and Jerry pulled him back.

Nancy's grip was beginning to weaken when she heard Sergeant Balsam say, "Okay, what's going on here?"

Just as he reached them, Susan stopped pulling away so suddenly that Nancy lost her grasp and fell back. Balsam put his hand on Susan's arm and repeated, "What's going on here?"

"I don't know, Officer," Susan said breathlessly. "I lost my balance and fell down, and the next thing I knew, Nancy Drew was grabbing my arm and twisting it."

Balsam turned his head. "Ms. Drew?" he said. "Do you have anything to say about this?"

Panting, Nancy fought to put the right words together. "Sergeant, if you'll search this woman I think you'll find—"

"Ms. Drew," Balsam cut in sternly. "I've given you a lot of cooperation, but I have to tell you—"

At that moment Nancy met Susan's eyes. The fear in them was evident. Even though Sergeant Balsam seemed reluctant to search her, Susan didn't think she had gotten away yet. Then Nancy noticed the odd way that Susan was holding her left arm. It was bent slightly and held pressed against her side.

Without pausing to think, Nancy reached out and yanked Susan's arm away from her side. Susan let out a scream as something fell from the inside of her parka onto the snow. Balsam was stepping forward to intervene when Nancy shouted, "There! Look! She had it inside her parka!"

On the snow at Susan's feet was a clear plastic sandwich bag. Through the plastic, rays of red and white fire gleamed. Susan had dropped the empress's jewels!

THE NANCY DREW FILES

A collective gasp rose from the crowd, followed by excited cries as everyone began to talk at once.

A horrified look came over Susan's face. For a fraction of a second, her eyes met Nancy's. She looked terrified and desperate. Making a quick, sudden turn, she tried to dash through the crowd to escape, but Balsam clamped a hand firmly around her arm.

With his free hand, the sergeant drew a card from his pocket and began to read, "'You have the right to remain silent . . .'"

Chapter

Sixteen

LATER THAT AFTERNOON, Nancy and her friends were gathered around the fireplace in Ned's frat house. Nancy was sitting on the sofa next to Ned, talking about the case and its solution.

"You mean Whorf denied knowing anything about the robbery?" Bess asked from her seat on the floor. She was propped against an oversize pillow in front of the fireplace.

Nancy nodded. "At first, Susan told the police that he didn't have a thing to do with it and that the robbery was entirely her idea."

"You don't sound as if you believed her," Jerry observed. He was standing next to the fireplace with his elbow on the mantel.

"No, I didn't. And thank goodness I was able to convince Susan to tell the police the *real* story when I went to visit her at the police station this afternoon."

Nancy stared silently at the flames for a few moments. Then she said, "Susan would steal the jewels if Whorf would agree to allow her father to stay independent and stop pressuring him to join his conglomerate. Whorf denied her story, of course. He maintained that she was working completely alone."

Rob was perched on the arm of George's chair. "I know Susan pretty well," he said. He paused to reach for George's hand. "I mean, I used to. She's too bright to go that far out on a limb without checking it out with Whorf ahead of time. Otherwise, how would she know which pieces of jewelry to steal, which ones Whorf most wanted to add to his collection?"

"You're absolutely right, Rob," Nancy told him. "Susan *was* smart—smart enough not to trust Whorf completely, even though they were working together. She tape recorded one of their conversations without his knowledge. When she played the tape for the police, that cinched the case against Whorf. He'll be going to jail, too."

Bess looked around at them and said slowly, "I kind of admire Susan. To risk everything to help her family—it can't have been easy for her."

Nancy held up a hand. "Now, wait a minute. Don't forget that she did her best to frame Rob for the theft." Turning to Rob, she added, "By the way, when I was talking to her at the police station, Susan told me that she hadn't originally intended to frame you—or anyone, for that matter. But when she went to set the boat house fire, she happened to spot you leaving the annex and start off on your run. Seeing that you looked upset, and that you didn't have your jacket, she saw her opportunity to set you up as the fall guy."

"And she also played a couple of very dangerous tricks on you, Nan," Ned added. "She may have some good points, but all in all, I'd have to say she's not exactly my favorite person."

Nancy sighed and leaned close against Ned. "She admitted that she locked me in the shed and removed the safety barriers from the lake.

"She didn't seem to know about my ski binding being tampered with, though," Nancy added. "My guess is that Whorf did that, although there's no way to prove it."

There was a short silence as everyone watched the dancing orange and yellow flames. After a few minutes Rob stood up and stretched.

"Don't forget, it's still Winter Carnival," he said. "I've got my old Flexible Flyer up in my room. Who's ready to take their chances on Suicide Hill?"

"That sounds terrific," George quickly said. "I love sledding."

Nancy glanced up at Ned, then said, "I think I'd rather take a walk."

Ned nodded.

"I'm going to sit by the fire awhile," Bess announced. "My toes still haven't thawed out from this morning."

"I'll keep you company, if you like," Jerry said, coming over to sit next to her.

As she and Ned set off hand in hand for a walk to College Woods, Nancy laughed softly.

"What's so funny?" Ned asked.

"Not really funny, just nice," she replied. "I'm just happy everything worked out so well."

"Sure," Ned said cheerfully. "Rob isn't in jail, the museum is out of hot water, the boat house didn't burn down, and I managed to dance with you twice last night before you went off detecting. What more could you ask?"

"This," Nancy said, turning toward him for a kiss.

After a long, breathless moment, Ned pulled gently away. "Here, I have something for you." He reached into the pocket of his parka and pulled out a small white box.

"Oh, Ned, you shouldn't have," she said.

There was a mischievous glint in his eye as he

told her, "Maybe you better open it before you thank me."

Shooting him a curious glance, she opened the small box, then laughed. A second later she lifted out a costume-jewelry necklace of red and clear glass set in fake gold. "It's perfect," she told him. "Right down to the 'Made in Hong Kong' stamped on the back!"

As he bent to kiss her a second time, she told him, "You can be sure this is one Winter Carnival I'll *never* forget!"

Nancy's next case:

Nancy's in Chicago to cheer the Emerson College basketball team, led by cocaptain Ned Nickerson, against their archrivals. But she can't believe her eyes. Has Ned saved his slickest moves for the post-game celebration? Is he really making a pass at Denise Mason, a cheerleader who bears a striking resemblance to Nancy?

The mystery takes an even more serious twist when a kidnapper, intending to abduct Denise, grabs Nancy instead! Denise's father is the curator of a museum, and a team of art smugglers are making a play for a priceless painting. In a case of forgery and mistaken identity, Nancy discovers that deception and danger are the only rules of the game . . . in *DON'T LOOK TWICE*, Case #55 in The Nancy Drew Files™.

Dear Friend,

Heard the latest? It seems just about everyone's talking about the sensational new series set in my hometown. It's called River Heights, and if you haven't heard, you don't know what you're missing!

You know I love to ask questions, so let me ask you a few. Do you like romance? A juicy secret? Do you believe there's life after homework? If so, take it from me, you'll love this exciting series starring the students of River Heights High.

I'd like you to meet Nikki Masters, all-American sweetheart of River Heights High, and Niles Butler, the gorgeous British hunk who makes Nikki's knees shake. And Brittany Tate, leader of the "in" crowd, who knows what she wants and will do just about anything to get it. She's got her eye on supersnob Chip Worthington. Samantha Daley, meanwhile, has fallen for Kyle Kirkwood. He's a social zero, but she's come up with a foolproof plan to turn him into the hottest ticket in town.

It's a thrill-filled world of teen dreams and teen schemes. It's all delicious fun, and it's all waiting for you—in River Heights!

Sincerely,
Nancy Drew

P.S. Turn the page for your own private preview of River Heights #9: *Lies and Whispers*.

Talk of the Town!

Brittany Tate, as devious as she is gorgeous, is out to snare the number-one country-club snob, Chip Worthington. He'd make the perfect boyfriend, her ticket to the top of the River Heights social scene. So what if she can hardly stand the guy?

Lacey Dupree can't forgive herself for the argument she had with boyfriend Rick Stratton just before his near-fatal rock climbing accident. Now that he's finally regained consciousness, the question that weighs most on her heart is, Will he ever forgive her?

Karen Jacobs has never loved any guy the way she loves Ben Newhouse. But the feeling can drive her to the depths of despair. Has Ben *really* gotten over his ex-girlfriend, model Emily Van Patten? And if not, how can Karen ever compete with someone so beautiful?

Ellen Ming is in trouble. Her father's been accused of embezzlement, and now Kim Bishop has accused Ellen of stealing junior class funds! Ellen's only hope is Nancy Drew. Will Nancy find a way to put a stop to the vicious gossip?

THE RUMORS ARE FLYING
IN RIVER HEIGHTS—
CATCH THEM IN
LIES AND WHISPERS!

"Hurry, Ben!" Lacey Dupree urged. "Can't you go any faster?"

"I'm doing the speed limit, Lacey," Ben Newhouse responded.

Lacey impatiently brushed back her halo of long red-gold waves and trained her eyes on the road ahead. Just one more block and they'd be at the hospital. One more block and she could see Rick Stratton, her boyfriend. Rick had finally regained consciousness after a rock-climbing accident.

Ben made a left turn into the hospital parking lot. Lacey opened her door as the car coasted to a stop.

"Whoa, Lacey!" Ben hit the brakes and turned to her. "I know you're anxious, but take it easy, okay?"

"I'm sorry, Ben," Lacey said as she opened the door wider. "I just can't wait. I have to see Rick!"

She slid out of the car and headed for the entrance. Across the lobby she skidded to a stop in front of the bank of elevators.

Jabbing the Up button impatiently, Lacey paused to

take a deep breath. Now that she was actually there, she started to worry again. What would Rick say when he saw her? He might hate her and blame her. If they hadn't had that terrible argument, he wouldn't have fallen during his rock-climbing expedition. He wouldn't have been lying unconscious in the hospital for more than two weeks!

The elevator doors slid open, and Lacey sprang on. She tapped her foot the whole time the elevator rose. As soon as the doors parted, she stepped out.

She thought of how she'd come there, day after day, her heart breaking at the sight of Rick lying unconscious. The pain of it had been hard to bear. But how would it compare to the pain of Rick's rejecting her now?

Rick's door was open. Lacey peeked in. Rick was pale, and there were dark circles under his eyes. His muscular body seemed thin now. He looked ill, Lacey thought, but he'd never looked so good to her.

He glanced up just then. "Lacey," he said.

"Hello, Rick." Lacey couldn't seem to move from the doorway. Did he want her to go to him? She didn't know what to do!

"Oh, Rick," Lacey whispered, her eyes blurring with tears. "I'm so glad you're back."

Couples! Everywhere Brittany Tate looked, she saw nothing but couples. When she got off the school bus, she almost crashed into Mark Giordano and Chris Martinez, king and queen of the jocks. Nikki Masters, the golden girl, was just pulling into a parking space with that adorable Niles Butler. From across the quad, Robin Fisher waved to Nikki and Niles with her boyfriend, Calvin Roth.

Brittany pressed her lips together as she headed up the walk. Robin had really spoiled things for her at the Winter Carnival Ball. She'd let Brittany have it for setting up a fight between Lacey Dupree and Rick Stratton. Robin had actually blamed Brittany for Rick's accident! It was bad enough that Brittany herself had felt guilty for her part in the couple's fight. She didn't need Robin to rub it in. And she certainly didn't need Tim Cooper to hear about it!

He'd been standing in the shadows, listening to every word. The rest of the night had been a disaster. Tim had been icily polite, but it was obvious he wished he was a million miles away. And he'd dumped Brittany on her doorstep like a load of old laundry.

She had come so close to having Tim for a boyfriend. She'd turned over a new leaf and been incredibly nice, and Tim had finally responded. But now Tim thought she was a double-dealing snake.

Brittany would never forgive Robin Fisher. Never. She gave Robin her trademark drop-dead look as she walked by. Robin merely grinned back at her. Brittany tossed her gleaming dark hair and hurried over to Kim Bishop and Samantha Daley, her best friends.

"What's going on with you and Robin?" Kim asked. "I saw that look you gave her."

Brittany shrugged. "That girl should get a life. She didn't like the fact that I went to the ball with her best friend's ex-boyfriend."

Samantha Daley leaned closer, her cinnamon eyes sparkling. "What *did* happen with you and Tim?" she asked in her soft southern drawl.

Kim and Samantha were staring expectantly. Brittany thought fast. She leaned over and said in a whisper, "I'll tell you a secret. That hunk Tim Cooper is just the teeniest bit boring. Nikki can have him." Brittany shook back her thick, dark hair and laughed. "I'm looking for someone a little wilder."

Normally, that comment would impress Samantha and Kim. They'd demand more details, wondering what she was planning. But Samantha and Kim were barely listening to her. They were staring over her head.

"Here come the guys," Kim said.

Brittany turned around. Jeremy Pratt and Kyle Kirkwood, Kim and Samantha's boyfriends, were heading for them. Kyle's face brightened at the sight of Samantha. Brittany wanted to throw up.

"Hello, gorgeous," Jeremy said to Kim. She smiled regally. The two of them were such a pain, Brittany thought impatiently. They thought they were the hottest thing to hit River Heights High since Mexican Day in the cafeteria.

"We were just talking about the country club dance this weekend," Jeremy said. "It's going to be major."

"It sounds okay," Kyle said. "I'm not a big fan of the country club, but Samantha really wants to go."

"I can't wait," Samantha said. She slipped her hand into Kyle's.

Brittany tuned them out. She was glad to be reminded of the country club dance. It would be the first big function she would attend as a member. It was time, Brittany decided, for her to be back on top. That meant snaring a fantastic new boyfriend.

"Who's going?" she asked Jeremy.

"Oh, the usual country club crowd," Jeremy said, waving a hand. "No one you'd know."

Brittany's hand tightened on her books. Jeremy

was so slimy he must have crawled out of a swamp. He never let her forget that she had only recently become a member—and only a junior member at that.

"Some of the college crowd will probably be there," Kim added.

Brittany sighed. "I'm sick of the college crowd," she said. "Jack Reilly called the other night, but I refused to speak to him. Who else is going, Kim?"

"The snobs from Talbot and Fox Hill, of course," Kim replied. Talbot and Fox Hill were the boys' and girls' private schools in River Heights.

"I just hope Chip Worthington isn't there," Jeremy muttered.

Brittany stifled a grin. Kim had told her that Chip had nearly rearranged the aristocratic Pratt profile a while ago. She could understand why Jeremy wouldn't want to see him again.

"You could always hire a bodyguard, Jeremy," Brittany said sweetly.

"It's not that I'm afraid of him," Jeremy returned quickly. "He makes all these comments about Kim, just to give me grief. He keeps leering at her and saying things like, 'What are you doing with the most beautiful girl in River Heights, Pratt?' Stuff like that. It's totally annoying."

"Really," Kim agreed, tossing her shiny blond hair.

Jeremy might hate it, but Kim wasn't too upset, Brittany was sure. Who wouldn't like being called the most beautiful girl in River Heights? Of course, Chip Worthington hadn't met Brittany Tate yet.

Then it hit her. Why not go after Chip? Brittany was bored with all the boys at school. Why not stake out some new territory? Let Kim and Jeremy be king and queen of River Heights High. Brittany and Chip would run the town!

Ellen Ming walked to the student council meeting. She took her usual seat and waited for Ms. Rose, the student council faculty advisor, to show up.

While she waited, Ellen began to feel uneasy. She saw Juliann Wade, the treasurer of the student council, whisper something to Patty Casey, who was the secretary. They both glanced at Ellen, then quickly looked away.

Ben Newhouse arrived, and then Kevin Hoffman came in. Kevin grinned warmly at Ellen as he slid into his seat.

Feeling a blush start on her cheeks, Ellen stared down at the tabletop. Sometimes the feelings she'd had when she had her crush on Kevin came back. Nothing had ever come of her silly crush, not even one date. Ellen knew she was too serious for Kevin, who was full of jokes and mischief. There was something about his unruly red-brown hair and easy grin that made her smile.

Ms. Rose walked into the room with her brisk step. "Good afternoon, people. Let's get started," she said. "Today the first item on the agenda is the proposal for a luau. A committee has already been formed, headed by Ellen Ming. Since the committee will be mainly using the decorations from the tropical theme that we scrapped for the Winter Carnival, the cost won't be too high. And the committee has high hopes that the record and tape sales will take care of the rest of the costs. Ellen, how's the whole plan going?"

"Fine," Ellen said. "We have volunteers lined up to handle the record and tape sales."

"Sounds great. Keep us posted," Ms. Rose said. She studied her notes again. "Now, if there's nothing else on the luau, let's get to—"

"Ms. Rose?" Juliann Wade waved her hand in the air.

Ms. Rose looked up. "Yes, Juliann?"

"I was wondering who's handling the proceeds from the record sale."

Ms. Rose frowned at Juliann, but she turned to Ellen. "Ellen?"

Ellen saw Patty Casey poke Juliann underneath the table. Ellen's heart began to flutter. "I am," she said in a shaky voice.

"What's your point, Juliann?" Ms. Rose asked frostily. Ellen had a feeling Ms. Rose knew what the girl was getting at—and she didn't like it.

Juliann shook back her blond hair defiantly. "I'm just wondering if we should reconsider having Ellen handle the funds, that's all. I'd be glad to take over."

"I agree with Juliann," Patty said quickly.

Ms. Rose studied the two girls. "And what exactly do you agree with, Patty?"

Patty's eyes traveled around the room as if she was seeking an answer. "Well, that maybe Juliann should take charge of the funds. She *is* school treasurer."

Juliann nodded. "Especially under the circumstances . . ." she said meaningfully, letting her voice trail off.

The room was quiet. Did that mean that people were shocked or that they agreed with Juliann? Ellen felt sick. How could this be happening? They thought she wasn't trustworthy enough to take charge of the money!

She felt Ben stir next to her, but before he could say anything, Kevin Hoffman spoke up.

"That's very nice of you, Juliann." Kevin's voice was calm, but it held a deadly undertone Ellen had never heard before. "Ellen *has* been doing two jobs since Lacey Dupree has dropped out temporarily. She could feel overloaded. I'm sure those were the circumstances you were talking about, right?"

Juliann swallowed. She glanced at Ms. Rose, who was giving her a cold stare. "Of course," she mumbled.

"But Ellen is doing such a fantastic job," Kevin went on steadily, "as usual, that as long as she feels she can handle it, I see no reason to make a change. Do you feel you can handle this on top of Lacey's responsibilities, Ellen?"

Ellen looked at Kevin. His green eyes had a fierce look. He nodded at her, giving her courage. He was on her side! "Yes," she managed to choke out.

"Then let's not waste any more time," Ms. Rose stated crisply. "We have more important business."

Everyone in the room relaxed, except for Ellen. Her heart was racing. Kevin had saved her neck, all right, but she couldn't get over the fact that Juliann had been so cruel in the first place.

Suddenly Ellen realized that she hadn't thought of the worst thing about her father's being accused of embezzlement. He might not go to jail, but his life still could be destroyed. He would always be under a cloud of suspicion.

Ellen had just seen something she wished she hadn't. People could take a rumor or a suspicion and they could use it to disgrace someone. If Ellen was facing that kind of attitude in a student council meeting, what would Mr. Ming face at work? Ellen shivered with foreboding. Things could get a lot worse before they got better.

Brittany scanned the crowd at the country club dance.

"Who are you looking for?" Samantha asked.

"I'm just shopping, Samantha dear," Brittany said distractedly. But just as she finished speaking, she caught sight of Chip Worthington. He was tall and seemed assured, as if he owned the country club. He scanned the room with a bored air.

Brittany willed him to turn around and look at her, but he turned his attention to his friends. She sighed. She'd have to get Kim to introduce her.

Brittany saw her chance. Kim and Jeremy were standing on the sidelines, having a soda. Brittany watched as Chip joined them. Jeremy's face darkened in a scowl, but Chip was grinning as he talked. He was probably tormenting Jeremy, Brittany thought. Maybe Chip wasn't so bad, after all.

Quickly Brittany walked across the room to Kim and Jeremy.

"Hi," she interrupted breathlessly. "I haven't had a chance to talk to you guys all night." She fixed her dark eyes on Chip. "Oh, I'm sorry, am I interrupting?"

"Not at all," Chip said. His clear green eyes flicked over her, and he gave a lazy grin. "Not at all," he repeated. "Who are *you,* and why haven't I met you yet?"

Brittany smiled back. "How about meeting me right now?" she said. "I'm Brittany Tate."

"Chip Worthington," Chip answered.

Kim stirred beside Brittany. She might not be able to stand Chip, but it was clear she didn't like Brittany stealing his attention, either. "Brittany became a junior member of the club recently," she said. "That's probably why you don't know her."

"I suppose you go to school with Pratt, here," Chip said. He casually ran a hand through his straight, side-parted brown hair.

"That's right. Do you go to Talbot?"

"Of course," Chip replied. "If every Worthington didn't enroll, the school would collapse and sink right into the ground. We practically built the place back in the Stone Age. Now we just throw pots of money at it to keep it running."

Brittany laughed her silvery laugh. What a snob! she thought. Kim was right, for once. "Well, thank heavens you enrolled, then," she said. "We wouldn't want anything to happen to Talbot."

"For sure," Chip agreed lazily. "And what do you do at River Heights High, Brittany?"

"Well, I'm on the school paper, the *Record,*" Brittany said. "I have my own column, called 'Off the Record.'"

"Nice name," Chip said.

Why did every remark he made sound as though he was making fun of her? Brittany wondered. But his eyes were definitely expressing approval. Did he like her or not?

Nikki Masters parked her car and followed Ellen Ming into the coffee shop. After they ordered sodas, Nikki looked at her expectantly.

"What's on your mind, Ellen?" Nikki leaned forward, her hands cupping her glass. Her blue eyes were kind and patient.

Ellen suddenly felt afraid. Nikki Masters had been in trouble once—that was true. But she was well past it now. She was beautiful and popular, and nice, too. Would she be able to sympathize with Ellen's problem?

"Ellen, if it makes it any easier for you, I know what it's like to need help," Nikki said softly. "I know it's hard to ask. But believe me, it's better. I want to do what I can."

Ellen's fears dissolved under the balm of Nikki's soft words. She gripped her glass and poured out her story, barely pausing for breath.

"I've gone over the junior class bank account more times than you can imagine," Ellen concluded. "I discovered right away that two deposits I recorded in the ledger didn't match the bank's record of deposits."

"How do you make the deposits?" Nikki asked. "At the bank?"

"No, it closes at three, so I use the night deposit slot," Ellen told her. "The two deposits were from last Friday and this Monday—from the record and tape sale. Each day I totalled the receipts, filled out a deposit slip, and sealed the envelope. Then I locked it in a drawer in the student council office. After school, I took it to the bank."

Nikki nodded thoughtfully. "So somebody got to the money while it was in the drawer. The person took out the bills and resealed the envelope.

"That's what I figure," Ellen said. "But, Nikki, who's going to believe that it wasn't me? After what's happened with my father, I mean."

"I believe it wasn't you," Nikki assured her. "Others will, too. Not everybody is like Kim Bishop, Ellen."

"But I'm class treasurer, Nikki. If my name isn't cleared, I'll lose the office."

"I have an idea," Nikki said slowly. "Would you mind if one more person knew the story? Not someone from school," she added hastily.

"Who?" Ellen asked, puzzled.

"Nancy Drew. She's a good friend of mine, and she lives next door."

"Wow," Ellen breathed. "Do you think it would be okay?"

"We won't know until I call her," Nikki said briskly. She reached into the pocket of her jeans for some change. "Can I?"

"Right now?" Ellen gulped. "I guess so. After all, how can I turn down a world-famous detective?"

Want more? Get the whole story in
River Heights #9, *Lies and Whispers.*